Disquieted Souls

Black Hills Wolves 29

By
Deena Remiel

Reviews for this book

This book touched my heart, made me cry, and had me smiling at the end! I couldn't ask for better than that!! ~ Amazon Reviewer

Romance, action and wolves! What more could you ask for? ~ Kristina's Books & More

A great read for a day when you can curl up with a cup of tea and get lost in a suspenseful paranormal romance ~ Amazon Reviewer

Fast paced, easy to read and exciting a great addition to the Black Hills Wolves ~ Amazon Reviewer

This is an inspiring tale about finding romance and your true place in life despite some real family and social issues that we have all faced ~ Amazon Reviewer

~A Note from the Author~

Welcome, Readers!

I'm so glad you've chosen to read *Disquieted Souls*, A Black Hills Wolves novel. I've a passion for writing about people who are broken in spirit. People who find their way to happiness and self-acceptance through the love and tender care of another. So, it is with great pleasure that I introduce you to Greyson and Willow, a couple whose disquieted souls are seeking to destroy their demons and find peace, love, and contentment in their lives. I hope their story tugs at your heartstrings and creates a lingering smile on your face when you're done.

Deena Remiel

Dedication

To my pack at home: David, and our two daughters.

Chapter One

Greyson slid his spent shot glass toward the edge of the bar counter. "One more, Gee, and make it a double."

His demand only bought him a disapproving glare from the self-righteous bastard. Well, maybe that was a little harsh. After all, he was one of a token few who didn't treat him like a pariah. Him and Drew, anyway. But such a look. He wasn't his father, although Gee'd practically raised his sorry ass from birth. So what if he wanted to get shit-faced after a long week of tracking? Surveillance could take a lot out of a man or Wolf.

"Gonna honor my request, my overly protective friend? My money's still good here, ain't it?"

"You'll have a hamburger and fried pickles with your alcohol."

"Yes, sir." He snickered and popped a toothpick

1

in his mouth to gnaw on.

He knew better than to argue with the old Bear and flashed him a toothy grin. His motto when it came to Gee? If he grinned at a bear long enough, the bear would eventually return the smile. He'd been grinning at the man for close to thirty years now, and he'd yet to see his goal realized. As the man of few words left to put in the order, Greyson hung his head. He almost never saw Gee at the bar, and he had to pick today to make an appearance. A week spent on edge, tracking an elusive rogue with no results to show for it, ruffled his fur something fierce. Lots of booze or a good screw would settle his disgruntled Wolf down. Seeing as no woman in the town would get within ten feet of him, he figured downing a couple of doubles, at least, were in his future.

He checked his reflection and then around the room through the mirrored backsplash behind the beer taps. There wasn't a person in the place who didn't look upon him as some kind of weird anomaly. For as long as he'd lived in Los Lobos, his unique appearance set him apart, and some made it quite clear his odd features made it uncomfortable to be around. Drew, Betty, Gee, and even Ryker were the only ones who'd seen past the pale skin and stark-white hair. Past the peculiar eyes—one indigo blue and the other amber with gold flecks. They saw right to the soul within.

As he'd grown, Greyson loved listening to Gee tell the story of how he came to be part of the Tao pack. He'd been left to die in the wilderness by a mother apparently not interested in caring for the runt of her litter. The Alpha's son, Drew, found him then Gee unofficially adopted him. As the two young boys grew up together, Drew would vehemently defend him against the other young ones in the pack, but it only seemed to exacerbate the teasing and relentless bullying by some when his friend wasn't around. Greyson realized soon enough he would have to stand on his own. His violent reaction to a bout of harassment scared the persistent young guns and served to finally put them in their place.

When he was old enough, he'd moved to the fringe of the pack lands, where he felt he wouldn't be subjected to any more possible taunts and jeers from bigoted Wolves on their way up the pack ladder. Of course, being a newly minted adult, he'd gotten resistance to break out on his own from Gee, but after Magnum expelled Drew, there was no reason to stay close to town. So he built a cabin on the very plot of land where he'd been dumped as a pup, hoping by living there he could someday learn of his mother's true motivations. A part of him hoped his birth pack lived somewhere nearby, and they'd show up one day for a reunion of sorts to put all his questions to rest.

Gee returned with a basket of fried pickles and a hamburger. He frowned and growled. "Eat."

"All right, all right. What about that drink?"

The were-bear grabbed the bottle of tequila and poured.

"Double, please. In fact, you know what? Just pour four shots-worth into a glass for me. Okay?"

He raised a brow, shook his head, but poured anyway.

"Thank you so much. Don't worry. I'll leave the way I came—running on all fours."

With a smirk and a snort, Gee turned on his heel and disappeared into the inner sanctum of his office. Of course, that left an opening for a group of idiots sitting at the table directly to Greyson's left to behave all sorts of stupid, making derogatory comments under their breath, but loud enough for him to hear. He'd never seen them in the bar before, but not recognizing them didn't mean anything. So many Wolves had returned home. If they were in Los

4

Lobos, Drew, Ryker and the others knew they were there. Self-consciously, he put his sunglasses on. Maybe giving them one less thing to comment on would make them move on to someone else.

With half a burger downed and a full glass of tequila tossed back, he was ready for their imminent attack. No sooner had he wiped his mouth with a napkin did they get up from their seats and approached. He breathed in slowly, deeply, deliberately to calm his ruffled Wolf.

"Hey, freak." The apparent leader of the pack of goons nudged his shoulder with a few fingers. He noted the latent strength in them but refused to respond in the hope they'd get bored and leave. "It's dark. Why you covering up them pretty eyes of yours?"

Though every fiber of his being thrummed and ached for him to let lose all the pent-up adrenaline on the asshole, Greyson didn't turn around, flinch, or remove his sunglasses, either. "Oh, I don't let just anyone gaze upon these beauties. I was waiting for you to come over here. These babies are for your eyes only, kitten."

That sparked a flurry of growls and snarls from the group, and the high-strung leader tossed a few chairs out of his way. The few other customers in the bar issued a collective warning growl. It was nice to know they were in his corner, should the need arise.

Greyson took his time and stood, showing the buffoons exactly what they were getting into. He stood a good head and shoulders taller than them and was nearly twice as wide. "Now before you go pouncing on me in that crazed, hormonal way of yours, let me tell you a little secret. You're in Gee's place. He doesn't take kindly to barroom brawls. Costs too much to fix and makes him a bit angry. So, if you wanna piss off the big old bear, go for it. In all honesty, if I were you, I'd leave *me* the fuck alone." He turned and then resumed his seat to finish his burger.

His assailants huffed and puffed as they surrounded him, and the first guy stuffed his pointed nose right up to Greyson's cheek. Through gritted teeth he hissed, "You're lucky, freak. This time. Next time, though, your ass is mine."

"My ass likes women. Sorry. But I think a few of your groupies might be into that kinda thing."

Another round of howling and Gee appeared with a bat in the doorway to the kitchen. The pack of idiots took the hint and left. He finished his burger, popped the last of the fried pickles in his mouth at a leisurely pace, and wiped his mouth again. Gee returned to the kitchen without a word. He'd give those jerk-offs a bit to clear out of town before he left for home. It wasn't a question of fear. He could easily obliterate each one of them without so much as blinking an eye. As a group, though, they were probably lethal.

The tequila finally kicked in and blunted his ability to absorb visual and auditory information. *Perfect. Now to head home and crash.* He tucked a few dollars under his glass and eased off the barstool, not sure if his feet would remember to move. He'd do much better to shift now. Four legs were better than two when he was drunk.

A simple shrug, like an involuntary shiver, then his clothes and body morphed into the Wolf who'd been denied the thrill of the kill all week long. With a gruff snuffle, he pushed the door open with his snout, looked all around with bleary eyes to check if the coast was clear before trotting down the dirt road, into the forest, toward his home.

As he loped along the winding path to the front porch, numbness crept across his haunches. It was only a matter of time before his legs followed suit. He shifted to his human form, took out his key, and unlocked the door after a number of failed attempts. As he poured himself into his bed, his last thoughts before passing out were, "Mission *not* accomplished. May you find the rogue fucker and kill him good and dead tomorrow."

***

It didn't take Willow five minutes to figure out the day's photo shoot was going to be a nonstop pain in the ass. Not only did the imbeciles at *Fashion Forward Magazine* contract two of the most annoying models, but the two most annoying models who couldn't stand each other. What were they thinking?

They weren't. They didn't give a rat's ass who slept with whom and then got dumped, or who had a restraining order against another. It came down to the almighty dollar. These models took phenomenal photos, so the fact they despised each other at the moment was irrelevant.

This week, Willow was stuck with the drama king and queen who never grew past their high school years. Carter and Cassandra were known to have been tight about a year before. After a few times catching him in bed with other models, she'd had enough and made no bones about spreading news of his philandering. Both held grudges forever. From the looks on their faces as they exited makeup and hair, today promised to be a grudge match for the ages.

Taking a deep breath and pretending not to notice, Willow headed toward the Fort Union Trading Post, a historic landmark in North Dakota and site for the day's fashion shoot. While waiting for the final touch-ups, a meadowlark flew past and landed on a light pole. She swung her camera up to her eye and focused in. Engrossed in her subject, only a harsh tap on her shoulder jolted her to reality. Her passion for nature photography would have to be sidelined until her day job released her.

"They don't pay you for lovely pictures of birds, Will. They pay you for lovely pictures of these two immature imbeciles of the human species. Come on."

"Can't say you don't speak the truth, Harry." Her lighting man laughed along with her as they made their way to the staging area.

Throughout the next three hours, she snapped hundreds of pictures, if not thousands, of Carter and

Cassandra looking hot, sexy, and posing in erotically charged positions for the swimsuit issue. In between shots, their hatred toward each other was palpable, but once the cameras were rolling, their sexually charged chemistry ignited the scene. That's how it'd been all week. Didn't matter where they set the backdrop. Nuclear war was imminent unless a camera was shooting.

"Two to one, those two will be fucking like bunnies at the end of this."

"Jesus, Harry! Could you be any *more* crass?" She took a long swig from her can of cola. "I wouldn't take that bet in a million years, though, 'cause I agree with you. Okay, folks! Break's over! Let's get this show on the road! I wanna see hot! I wanna see sexy! I wanna feel as though there's no way I could ever walk down a beach or swim in a pool or even walk into a...a trading post without wearing one of those swimsuits! Go!"

When the last shot had been taken, everyone clapped and hugged. She even got hugs and a comment from Cassandra. "You are one of the best photographers we've ever worked with. It's been a great week overall, for sure, but we're exhausted. So glad it's finally over."

The greatest you've ever worked with? That's because every time you objected to something, which was every freakin' shot, I had to comply with your wishes, as per my supervisor's directive, you immature brat. Or, I could've ignored you and lost my job.

"Any time! Good luck with your next job. See you around." She flashed a courteous grin, calculating how fast she could get out of there. As she packed up her gear, she heard a racket from the makeshift dressing room. She laughed and shook her head. It never ended! With her bags and lighting safely stowed, she hopped in her SUV and shoved off. In her rearview mirror she watched as Carter and Cassandra ambled out of the dressing room a bit mussed and arm in arm. The tabloids were gonna have a field day with the latest development.

Back in her motel room, with a poor excuse for takeout pizza resting on the bed and a cold beer on the bedside table, Willow rested her weary bones and closed her eyes. It wasn't that she was tired from the day's work. She was exhausted from all the bullshit she'd had to put up with since landing this gig. When she'd first started in the fashion photography business, she didn't notice all the nuances of relationships and political power plays. That was four years ago. Now, at twenty-eight, she was burned out and ready to give it all up. Admittedly, her life was deep in the crapper, and she struggled with how to crawl out. If she had to bartend to make ends meet, she would.

She sat up tall, her hooded eyes snapped wide open, her brain, instantly alert with equal parts excitement and horror. "I do believe...I've decided...I might be done with this bullshit career." The thrill of a possible change set her heart racing and mind on full-tilt. *What exactly am I saying here?* "Whoa, whoa, whoa, my dear, let's not make any rash decisions. Sleep on it. Take a break. You're due for a vacation anyway. See how you feel when you return. Right? Right." The fashion industry, with all its plastic models and phony, two-faced people would still be there when she returned. *If* she returned.

She chomped down on a doughy slice and took a long draw of beer. Yeah, that decision sat well with her. There was nothing pressing at home in California. No animals to look after. Her parents were traipsing through Africa for the year, and her brother and sister were workaholics. No jobs coming up for her until next month. It was the perfect opportunity to go off the grid, relax, reevaluate her life, and nurture her passion by taking as many pictures as she wanted of nature.

She leaped off the bed and grabbed her laptop to search for places to camp. She'd had enough of North Dakota, so she went south with her search. South Dakota had the Black Hills National Forest. They had campgrounds where she could pitch a tent or set up an RV. Within the hour, she had reservations for four weeks starting the next day. Now all she needed was the equipment and gear to set up her home away from home. She'd pick them all up, along with the pull-along pop-up camper, once across the state line at an RV rental center.

Camping and hiking were second nature to her. She'd done all sorts with her family for years from tent to camper, even survivalist style. She picked off a piece of pepperoni from the last slice. As she popped it into her mouth, she recalled a fond childhood memory, when they attempted to make pizza over a campfire. Her parents had their moments of coolness. Not many, but a few. Once they and her siblings scattered across the fifty states and explored more urban pursuits, she still had the rugged bug deep inside her and managed to continue camping on her own, but never for this long. *This is gonna be one hell of an adventure!*

The next morning, she awoke with the sun and got an early start on her trek to the other Dakota. A stop at the local Laundromat gave her time to eat some breakfast with Harry first.

"You're really doing this?"

"Yes, I really am." She folded a piece of bacon into her mouth, talking as she chewed. "It's no big deal. I'm a longtime hardcore camper, my friend."

"But for a month? You're a strange bird."

"Honestly, I've never camped for this long, but I'm sure it'll be fine. I'll be taking as many pictures of those dang birds as I want, by the way. And elk and rabbits and trees and insects and...."

"I get it. I get it! You want to be one with nature."

"No, I just want to take pictures of it. I don't mind living beside nature, though. It's a far cry from those neurotic, infantile people we have to deal with day in and day out. Harry, I gotta do this or I'll lose my soul. It's practically gone as it is. I barely recognize who I am anymore."

He reached out a hand to cover hers and squeezed. "So, do you need me to do anything while you're Grizzly Willow?"

She rolled her eyes. "Actually, yes. Just one thing. Can you mail this rent check out for me on the date I wrote on the envelope? I don't think I'll be anywhere near a post office."

"Sure, no problem."

She tapped her napkin against her lips and placed it on the remains of her pancakes. "Well, I gotta run. Laundry's probably done, and they're the only clothes I have."

They stood at the same time and hugged hard. She didn't have close friends. Who did in the fashion industry? But Harry was as close as she'd get. "Listen, if you need anything, call me. Don't let your phone's battery run out. You hear me?" She nodded. "And if it gets too much, haul your ass home."

"Got it. Thanks so much for everything, Harry. You're the only *real* person I know in this crazy, effed-up business. Promise you'll remember to keep it real. All right?"

"Promise." One last hug and she left him to finish his coffee.

Clothes were scorched dry and ready for folding. She placed them right into her suitcase, zipped it up, and called the RV place where she reserved the latest model of a small pop-up camper equipped with a sink

15

and a double-burner stove. She'd be living in style in the Black Hills of South Dakota!

Chapter Two

Willow had her choice of spacious, "newly renovated" campsites, whatever *that* meant. She looked on the map provided by the burly, weathered manager on duty and chose the one most remote from all others.

"Now, I can't assure you no one will wind up camping next to you." He dug into a bag of tobacco, took out a clump, and shoved it between his cheek and gum. "But I have no one scheduled at the moment."

"I appreciate it and understand. As long as I can get a few days of utter human silence, I think I'll survive."

He spat into a cup. She fought not to grimace and brought a hand up to hide a cough.

"Rough time of it?"

17

"I work in the fashion industry as a photographer, so there's always a rough time of it even when there shouldn't be."

"Oh, yeah well, I hear those people have lots of trouble with low self-esteem and all."

"You don't know the half of it. So, one last thing before I head out. Is there a bathroom facility with a shower?"

"Yes, the closest one is about a two-minute walk from your site. It's marked on the map there."

"That'll do. And you say there's a stream near me?"

"Yes, ma'am. In my opinion, you have the prettiest spot out of all the ones I got."

"Can't wait to see it. I believe you gave me everything, and I paid. I think I'm ready to go find my space and my peace. Thank you for everything."

"My pleasure." He spat again. "Enjoy your stay."

"Oh, without a doubt." She knocked a determined fist against the burnished counter then turned around to leave. *No turning back now, lady. You're all paid up and have a place to squat. Make the most of it.*

Over bumpy, dirt roads and through an overgrowth of brush, she finally arrived at her new

18

home. She turned off the car, sat for a moment, then jumped out and ran around the space, hooting and hollering as though she was a woman wrongfully imprisoned and set free. The way she saw it, she was. So discontented with her life, this silly vacation was a game-changer.

Her SUV and the pop-up fit perfectly in between the mature pine trees, with enough shade to keep the truck cool. Once officially parked, she popped up the camper and set up her new living quarters. It was one adorable little thing and suitable for her needs. It even had a new camper smell. Fire wasn't essential since she had a cooktop inside, but it was a great aesthetic and could always help her in a pinch.

As she gathered the kindling and firewood, she recalled the time she was given the nickname Firestarter. Her parents held a contest between the children to see who could make fire the fastest. She snickered. With them, *life* was a competition. Since she'd won, she was given the name and was called it whenever they went camping from that point on. No surprise then her siblings rallied and vied to be the best at everything else, always at her expense. *What a way to grow up—being bested by your family morning, noon, and night.* That kind of mental conditioning set her up for many therapy sessions.

That was the past. She saw her family every couple of years at the most, if she had to. Back to the present, she had the fire started in a blink of an eye, using her favorite method, the teepee. It helped that the campsite already had fire rings set up and ready for users.

The flames licked the small logs, and she equated it to her job—so enticing at first, but, over time, blackened one's soul. Hers was pretty charred at the moment. With the fire managed, she took a stroll by the stream and dipped her feet in the brisk mountain water. She closed her eyes, breathing in deep the strong scent of pine and clean air. It didn't take long for her surroundings to seep into the nooks and crannies of her depressed, unfulfilled heart, to smooth out the rough edges. It came as no surprise. Being out in nature always soothed her.

With a clear head, she rolled around ideas for her next steps and whether a change of career was something she could seriously consider. Salary was a huge stumbling block. She made enough money to live, but not enough to pay any kind of attention to her true love: nature photography. Could she, at this point, give up the fashion industry and find a job paying well enough to support her passion? Could she focus all her energies of making a go at nature photography alone with no other job? The times she'd entered her photos to contests through *National Geographic*, they were well received. She'd even won. So, she always would send her photos when she could to keep her name in front of the right people.

During her time in the Black Hills, she would take as many pictures as possible. She wanted to tell stories with a deer's eyes or an insect's journey up a tree or a raindrop hanging on for dear life at the end of a leaf. She wanted to capture the magic of nature and in a way no one had seen before. But could she making a living from it? Only time would tell. What would be her fallback plan? No doubt, she'd have to return to her job at *Fashion Forward Magazine* or find some other one with comparable pay. Reality said, fat chance. If there was any bigger motivation to make her passion work as her career, this was it.

As she slipped her shoes on, the urge to start immediately forced her body into action. The sun was going down. She scurried back to camp to grab her pack filled with orienteering gear, a bottle of water, her hat with a headlamp, and her camera bag. The hiking map showed a clearing west of her site, a perfect spot to set up her camera for sunset pictures. She locked the door to her camper and truck, and trudged through the unfamiliar terrain, exhilaration pulsing strong in her chest from the unknown. It'd been a long while since she had to rely on her skills to find her destination without the benefit of help from others, and a horde of tiny butterflies took up residence deep in her belly.

Her hike led her through some densely forested areas, making the trek slower than she'd have preferred. She climbed over fallen tree trunks, balanced across others, and, at times, had to divert her course to go around the massive overgrowths of giant knotweed, which put a bit of a cramp in her style. Good thing she was also an expert at orienteering. A straight path to the clearing would only happen if the forestry service were to clear it. As it stood, a winding, treacherous path was more the order of the day.

Finally, she found the perfect spot and any lingering annoyance faded away. The surrounding vistas more than made up for the journey and would probably feed her soul throughout her return to base. She could see for miles to the deep green rolling hills, craggy stone outcrops, and the sky layered with clouds of magenta, peach, and violet. She dropped everything and grabbed her camera. Soon enough, its clicking blended with the chirping of the birds and hissing of the insects. The sky, the mountains, the life teeming around her, all stepped up to the plate in a spectacular display for her.

No sooner had she begun documenting the wondrous event than it was over. The sun had set. Satisfied with the day's efforts, and exhausted by all she'd accomplished, she journeyed to her campsite for a dinner of franks and beans, and to collapse in front of the fire.

***

A full-body shiver roused Willow from a blizzard-filled dream. No wonder. It was fucking freezing! She'd fallen asleep by the fire, now only embers, wearing only shorts and a T-shirt. Nighttime temperatures dipped below comfortable up in the mountains. She'd known and should've taken two seconds to change before sitting down to eat. What good would it do for her to get sick on the first day of vacation?

"Son of a bitch, it's cold!" She hustled inside the camper and rummaged through her bag of clothes. With quaking hands, she managed to pull a sweatshirt over her head and exchange her shorts for jeans. Calmer, warmer, she returned to the dying fire and put it out of its misery. Wide awake, she pondered what to do. She could do anything, really. Read, write, listen to music, or take nighttime shots of nocturnal animals.

"Camera, it is!" She changed over the filter and lens to accommodate the darkness, and decided tonight she'd make a circle about the campsite. She gave herself a fifty-foot radius in any direction. She'd widen the circle in the days to come. With LCD flashlight in one hand and camera in the other, she trudged through the undergrowth hoping to document a nighttime rendezvous with any critter willing to mug it up for the camera.

Two hours and nothing. Not a single ant would grant her even half a smile. Deflated and bored, she turned back toward the camper. "Tomorrow is another day, you know. And you have about twenty-nine more of these to come. Best to get some rest, my dear. And maybe you should work on not talking to yourself out loud. The animals might think you're crazy."

***

After two days of getting to know her surroundings and animal neighbors, Willow ventured to unfamiliar territory. At sunrise, she packed a bag with water and energy snacks and headed east. The changes that washed over the landscape as the sun rose higher in the sky stole her breath away. What the shadows hid, the sun revealed. What was once right there before her eyes then disappeared. To capture the subtle changes in hue, she fixed her camera on a continuous setting. At the very least, she'd make a killer video of the ever-shifting nature of the land as it awakened.

She returned to base by noon, had a hearty lunch and reloaded, then headed west to make the most of the afternoon sunlight. The area she'd found was crawling with wildlife of all kinds—elk, rabbits, birds, creepy-crawly things, not to mention the variety of flora. On sensory overload and confounded on what to shoot first, she closed her eyes to calm down.

What should I focus on? What's grabbing my attention? There's a rabbit with a chunk bitten out of

25

its ear. I could follow him. Do it.

She settled in a good hundred yards from the rascal and started shooting, narrowing the focus to its mouth nibbling at a leaf, then shifted to its shredded ear flopping about in the breeze. *Lucky fella! I wonder what got a piece of you.* As she continued to click, a sudden rustling to her left froze the rabbit in its place. Its ears twitched and moved like a satellite dish finding its signal. Through her eyepiece, she scanned the underbrush and fixated on a pair of unsettling eyes. Black pupils surrounded by a circle of rich amber penetrated the dense forest growth, eyeing its prey. A mountain lion had chosen rabbit for dinner this evening, and her heart lurched realizing it easily could have been her he'd set his sights upon. Not so lucky a little fella anymore!

Torn, she continued to photograph the big cat as it stalked ever closer to the oblivious rabbit, who'd picked up where it left off, munching leaves. *This is nature. Survival. But why did something so darn cute have to die?* And yet, better *it* than her for the lion's dinner. The predator moved in for the assault, and the poor rabbit didn't stand a chance. The feline pounced without hesitation and bit the little bugger's neck. So violent, so quick, Willow's blood shushed in her ears as her heart thumped wildly. She prayed she captured it all and that at least one picture would be decent. The mountain lion loped off with the rabbit still in its mouth, and she breathed for the first time in what felt like a million years.

Daylight dimmed, and with it drained all the adrenaline fueling her to spend another hour taking every possible picture, flora and fauna. Weariness set in, so she headed for dinner and an evening of relaxation. When the moon was high and bright, she'd go on another night hunt, foraging for those elusive, one-of-a-kind opportunities that would prove she had the chops to make it in the nature photography industry.

"Shit! Shit! Shit!" She'd thought the path clear, but a branch of sneaky stinging nettles played dirty in the darkness and entangled itself in Willow's shirt. It wouldn't let go for love nor money. None of the sharp hairs had touched her skin yet, but if she wasn't careful, they could, and it wouldn't be pleasant. She stopped any movement, took a deep breath, and weighed her options.

She could try to remove the bastard weed from her shirt, but she'd run the risk of being touched by the poisonous hairs. Or, she could remove her shirt. Neither was desirable, but she needed to do something. She couldn't very well stand there all night on some godforsaken path to nowhere. *Leave the damn shirt! It's cold, but not cold enough to get hypothermia.* She wasn't far from camp, maybe a fifteen-minute walk. So, she extricated herself from the long-sleeved T-shirt and left it for the weeds to consume. Goose bumps raised the hairs on her arms, and when her teeth chattered, she picked up the pace to generate some heat.

Within ten minutes, she recognized the welcome glow of the lantern she'd left on by one of the pop-up's windows. Relief washed over her, flooding her body with artificial warmth. Snarls and growls stopped her dead in her tracks and sent her heart plummeting to the pit of her stomach. High-pitched whines and yaps were followed up with more growling and scrabbling.

Coyotes? Wolves? And where the hell were they? Close. Too damn close.

Using her flashlight, she scanned the most direct route from where she stood to her camper. Nothing stood in her way. Except abject fear. Her feet glued themselves to the forest floor. The chaos scraped away at her nerves, and she covered her ears as the skirmish seemed to be getting closer.

Damn it, girl! Get the fuck back to the camper!

Sheer determination not to die alone broke her feet free, and she ran, full-speed, only to fumble with the camper's door. Once inside, she locked it, knowing it was foolish to think such a poor excuse for a lock could protect her. But, at least, she wouldn't be seen. She threw on her sweatshirt and hunkered down.

The brawl had definitely moved closer, so close she could hear the vicious snapping of teeth and scrabbling of paws against the dried pine needles. Horrified, all she could do was pray they wouldn't use her site as their final battleground.

One pain-filled yowl and the snarls turned to howls and barks. More importantly, they receded. The pack of wolves, most likely, had taken off to wherever the next bit of fun lay. They had their fill of ruthless violence then ran off. What kind of animals would do that to another? Ones who would do anything to protect their territory or to settle a score.

Whatever they massacred, though, was still near. Whimpers, almost like human sobs, wormed its way into her heart. The poor animal was in dire pain and probably dying a slow death. Her so-called friends in the real world would call her melodramatic, but she'd never heard anything so heart-wrenching in her life.

She couldn't bear listening to the abject agony any longer, and a thought crossed her mind. What if she did a photo essay using this wounded animal as the subject? It would satisfy so many things: her curiosity, her need to help, and her desire to photograph something unique and gritty.

Determined and resolute, she gathered her camera, switched out the lens and filters, and stuffed a pocketknife in her pocket. Flashlight on, she stood on the step of the camper and listened. The whimpers seemed to come from her right, so she journeyed out of her safe haven in search of the wounded animal. She wouldn't get too close. Just enough to get those money shots.

She'd gone fifty yards from the fire ring when she came upon a mess of fur and matted undergrowth. Only fifty yards! No sign of the wounded, though. Another, much weaker whine and snuffle filled the air directly before her. Instinct told her to run for safety.

Her soul refused.

She crouched down low and inched closer, using

the small shrubs to hide behind. Peeking around one, she sucked in a breath. Her eyes were met with a most extraordinary and appalling sight. On the ground, in a heaving mass, lay an enormous white wolf, its fur streaked with blood, tufts strewn about. Its eyes weren't closed, but they weren't quite open either. Willow gripped her stomach, where a horrid ache had welled, and swiped at tears she hadn't realized had fallen. Blurred vision wouldn't help with snapping shots.

She lifted the camera to her face and began documenting the wolf's demise, but no sooner had she begun, then her conscience brought up a moral dilemma. Shouldn't she help it, rather than immortalize its death?

Just a few more pictures, and I'll put the camera down and do something.

As she looked through the eyepiece, she zoomed in. They hadn't marred the face. Its stomach raised and lowered at a very slow pace, and the majority of the wounds, gashes mostly, were inflicted there and on its hindquarters. They'd not gone for the kill. They'd inflicted a good deal of maiming, though. She shook her head. Her remarks sounded as though she were assessing the injuries of a man who'd been jumped on the streets.

She slung the camera strap across her shoulder and to one side, then approached, feeling a bit more at ease since the wolf was very much unconscious. It was time to do something to help it out. She needed to get a much closer look to see what she could use from her emergency first aid kit. Hers was not the standard, garden variety, either. After years of camping and learning absolutely anything could happen, she created a tailor-made one rivaling the urgent care facilities. She never left home without it.

Reaching out a tentative hand, she trembled as it touched the soft fur low on its belly. Oddly enough, the animal seemed familiar as if she'd been connected to it in some way. Preposterous thought, yet the feeling persisted. She marveled at the denseness while gingerly moving it aside to get a better look. Fresh blood oozed from a set of slashes needing suturing. If she could be sure it wouldn't awaken during the process, she'd do it in a heartbeat. As it stood, it wasn't wise. She moved on to examine the leg. It was pretty torn up, too.

As she pondered her limited options on how to help without getting herself killed in the process, the wolf's body seemed to waver and shimmer. Like a crab, she scurried behind a bush and raised her camera to her eye to get a better look at the peculiarity. Her finger instinctively pressed down for continuous drive mode while her jaw dropped in awe. If these pictures didn't come out, she'd hang up her camera bag for the rest of her life. Right before her eyes, the wolf morphed into a human male! Had she not been so shocked and intrigued, she would have blinked and missed the change completely, as the entire shift took all of five seconds. Wasn't this the stuff of horror movies and nightmares? If so, why wasn't she frightened?

Those golden moments were captured on a whole string of photographs. Without a moment to fully absorb the implications of what had occurred, Willow now had a whole new set of issues to confront. There was a man, badly wounded and unconscious, lying in shredded clothes on the ground. Would he be as lethal as a wolf if he awakened while she treated him?

She chose to believe not. Although the potential was undeniable given the size of this total stranger. She could throw "human" out the window, too. Shoving all logic and sense to the side, she swung into action. An injured "something" needed help. Period.

The end. She ran with her camera in hand to the camper, and returned with rope to help her haul the massive man and all his unconscious dead weight to the fire ring. He was in seriously poor shape considering all the grunting she did and he didn't even stir or respond with groans of his own. Before beginning, she downed an entire bottle of water and doused her head with a cool stream of the stuff despite the frigid evening temperature. If a strong woman contest were ever to be created, she proved she could be a top contender.

With his jeans cut away on his right leg, she bristled. He'd have severe scarring, not to mention permanent muscle damage. His upper thigh resembled a pound of ground beef. They'd left nothing to sew up. She thanked God he remained unconscious because the pain would be excruciating as she washed out the dirt and debris and covered it with antibiotic ointment and lots of soft gauze. The healing of the area would not be pleasant.

Moving on to his other injuries, she lifted his tattered T-shirt and cut the final thread away to have a fresh look at the gashes now that he was man, not wolf. There were five on the left side of his abdomen and five more on the right. All ranged anywhere from three to six inches long. Some were shallower than others, so, after cleaning those wounds, she used butterfly tape wherever she could, stitched up the rest, and covered it all with more gauze and tape.

"Damn good thing I was around, otherwise you would've died from bleeding out or infection." She knew he couldn't hear her, but talking out loud while she poked a needle through the flesh of a man who'd been a wolf only a short time ago helped keep her calm. "This ought to get you well on your way to being fine. And when you wake up, you can go to a hospital where they can check out my handiwork."

Once done, she washed her hands with antibacterial soap and took in her first full breath since the whole ordeal began. "Nothing left to do now but keep an eye on him and rest. Right. Like I'm gonna close one flipping eye while he's here."

Her camera sat on the counter, a voiceless beacon of information. Dare she look at the photos of him...it? She had to. Just to be certain she wasn't hallucinating during a period of heightened emotional distress. She turned the camera on and hit the Menu button to start the picture review. Looking at the pictures in reverse order, the man turned into a wolf. Forwarding through, he shifted into a man.

Deep breath in. Deep breath out. Slow your heart before it smashes through your chest. Over and over, Willow scanned back and forth, watching wolf become man and man become wolf. Incontrovertible evidence now existed, and it was right in her sweaty palms. Werewolves were real!

In all the horror movies she'd watched growing up, they were violent, ruthless killers and lacked any kind of self-control. But, there were novels she'd read, too, where they were quite heroic, protective, and oozed sexual confidence. All were fictional. So, with reality hitting her square in the jaw, what would this werewolf be like?

"Seems like a good time for an ice-cold beer." She popped the top on a can before returning to the fire to sit by her wounded charge. She raised it in salute.

"Cheers to you, Lon Chaney." Taking a long sip, she then burped and continued. "So, who are you, really? Why did they do this to you? Doubt you're gonna tell me a damn thing when you wake up."

Goose bumps appeared on his skin.

"We don't need you getting cold now." She hurried into the camper and returned with a sleeping bag. "All right, now, you stay put, and I'll move

36

whatever part of you needs moving." She scrunched up the cocoon-like bag and stuck his feet in first, then scooted it over and under the rest of his body until she ran out of material. That happened when she reached his ribs. She took hold of his arms and tucked them into the bag, too. "Well, at least your wounds are covered. Your chest on up is gonna have to deal with the cold."

Wide awake, curious as hell, and inexplicably drawn to him, she examined the puzzling man's exposed features. If the sleeping bag were long enough, his shoulders still wouldn't fit. They were far too broad, and she couldn't stop herself from following the hills and valleys of his muscles. She already knew how muscular the rest of him was from tending to his thigh wound. Ashamed of her ogling, she cleared her throat, took another swig of beer, and moved on with her "clinical" observations.

His face, at rest, was an exquisite example of strong male features—squared jaw, high cheekbones, strong brow, Roman nose. In concert, they presented a formidable facade. His lips, thick and strawberry red, were in stark contrast against his pale skin, the palest she'd ever seen. But the most striking feature so far was his pure white hair, thick and straight, falling like icy blades of grass to brush against his shoulders. Her fingers ached to run through it and wind the luscious strands around each one. She bit her bottom lip, as her breath hitched, and sat on her hands for good measure. *What about his eyes? Will they be as alluring and enigmatic?*

As the thought struck, they opened. Not with a flutter. Not like someone roused from sleep. They had been closed, and then they were...open and staring into hers. Her ass dropped to the ground and she gasped from the sheer awkwardness of the moment.

Gathering her wits, and thinking he'd probably be confused as hell, she righted herself and spoke quickly to avert any unease. "Don't be afraid and don't move too much. My name's Willow Bisset, and you've been badly injured on your stomach and thigh. I cleaned you up and dressed your wounds, but you'll want a professional to take a look, maybe give you a tetanus shot if yours isn't up to date." She offered a tentative smile. *What the hell am I babbling on about?*

"How bad?" His gravelly whisper barely reached her ears.

She pressed her lips together and rolled them

between her teeth. *What to tell him? What to tell him?* Did she give him the blunt truth of it or sugarcoat? He didn't seem the sugarcoat type, so she barreled ahead. "Your thigh's mashed up pretty badly. I'm afraid there might be lingering muscle damage. Your stomach has a variety of gashes I've sewn up or butterfly taped together. About ten in all. I didn't see any other wounds."

He rolled his head away from her. "Son of a bitch."

"I figured I'd go to the manager's office in the morning and ask him to get an ambulance sent to take you to the hospital."

"No!" He quickly snapped his head around toward her, and, if looks were bullets, she'd be dead. "No hospitals. No doctors."

She instinctively leaned away. Some people hated hospitals. Others hated doctors. So he was both. Or.... A sick feeling crept under her skin as another option she hadn't considered fed into growing paranoia. "Okay then, none of that." She paused, wondering how wise it was to ask the next question, but she had to. "Are you a fugitive from the law?"

He bared a perfect set of pearly white teeth any

mother would be proud of and chuckled. "No. And I've never been arrested, either. You can relax."

"So," she pressed on, breathing easier once again, "you have a thing against the medical profession?"

He turned his face toward her, and she could now confirm his eyes, one rich amber with golden flecks, the other the deepest blue, were as beguiling as she'd figured. "You could say I'm a fast healer. I'll be fine in a couple of days...Willow."

When he spoke her name, it was as though he'd spread a coat of silky chocolate over her entire body and licked every ounce of it off with his tongue. Her palms tingled, her face flushed, and she shifted in her seat to ease the growing ache down low.

"Fast is one thing, but you'd need to be supernatural to bounce back from these wounds in a couple of days. Insert foot in mouth, Will." She groaned and dropped her head into her hands.

"What do you mean?" His voice returned to a shaky whisper, but she heard him just fine.

She shrugged off her embarrassment and peered up at him. Enough dancing around the issue. She needed answers now that he was conscious and looking all delicious despite his injuries. So, she ignored his question and asked the first of many of her own. "Who are you?"

"My name is Greyson. Thanks for fixing me up. I'm sure you did an awesome job."

"You're welcome. I'm no doctor, but I make a damn good triage nurse in the wilderness when I need to. Back to you, Greyson. *What* the hell are you? And what actually happened out there? I can only guess, but I want the whole story. From the beginning. I don't think it's too much to ask...considering."

"What if it *is*?"

"What if it is *what*?"

"Too much to ask."

Stunned, she'd hoped he would've shared something to appease her. The tiniest bit of information. She did save his life, after all. And yet, she understood. "You're protective of your privacy."

"I have to be."

"Not around me, you don't."

"Why not?"

"I found you, Greyson. And when I found you, you were, well, you were...a wolf." She sat holding her breath, wondering how he'd react. Amidst groans and yelps, he tried worming his way out of the sleeping

41

bag. She pressed her hands against his chest to ease him back down. "Oh no, you don't, mister. You're staying put. You're in no shape to go anywhere."

"You're batshit crazy, lady, if you think I'm a wolf, and I don't need to be hanging around any insane people." He tried again to get up, but his leg wouldn't cooperate.

"I'm not crazy, and you're going to tear open all those stitches I put in ya if you keep this up." She settled him down and fluffed the sleeping bag. "I know what I saw. Aren't you the least bit curious why I'm still here and didn't leave you to die out there? I'm sure as hell curious about you. You say it'll take a couple of days to heal. We have plenty of time to get to know each other."

"I don't want to know you. And you shouldn't want to know me, either. In the morning, I'm outta here."

She stood up and dusted off her pants. "Well then, don't let the tree branches hit you in the ass on your way out. Good night." She smirked and tromped off to her camper, where she slammed the door shut and locked it. "And good riddance."

Turning off the lantern, Willow crawled onto her bed and groused. How rude! One lousy comment about him being a wolf and he clammed up. She punched her pillow, hoping to fluff it. It stayed sunken with her fist's imprint. She sighed. Did he really think calling her crazy would work? She had photographs, proof! Those pictures would catapult her into the stratosphere of prizewinning photojournalism. Yeah, she'd keep that little morsel to herself.

When the morning came, she hoped to find him long gone. After lying to herself, she crashed and fell into a series of B-movie dreams where vampires and werewolves fought for her soul. Werewolves were winning when she stirred awake with the birds' morning songs.

Chapter Three

The sleeping bag rested on her doorstep, neatly rolled and secured. *Now he's courteous? And, damn it, he's gone.* Disappointment continued to war with intrigue and perplexing, unrequited desires. After scrubbing the pan of stuck-on scrambled eggs, she went on to obliterate the nonstick surface. What kind of wonderland had she fallen into at this campsite? And what the hell was she doing, being so sexually drawn to one of its fantastical beasts? There was no explanation for it.

Greyson was right. She'd gone batshit crazy. And there wasn't a damn thing she could do about it except give herself time to get over it and join the real world again.

Grabbing her camera, she removed the SD card. It needed to be separated from the others and secured from possible thieving hands. Her camera bag was too obvious a hiding spot, socks could be easily thrown in the wash, and her makeup bag would destroy it. So, where to stow it? She settled on a sandwich baggie placed in a zippered compartment in her purse, one she never used.

"Time to focus on something new and preferably nonsupernatural!" She clapped her hands together and headed out the door with a fresh SD card in her camera, hat and sunglasses, and a compass and water bottle.

Traipsing along the forest floor, she stopped and turned her camera downward. A parade of industrious ants was hard at work, carrying all manner of food. She followed them for quite a distance, being careful not to get bitten or in their way, until they disappeared under a rotted log. Moving on to spy something else, she loved how the dappled sunlight cast an ethereal glow about her, so she stopped to capture the beauty. Butterflies fluttered lazy paths between leaves high in the canopy. Birds flitted from tree branch to branch and sang to each other. It seemed the closest to the Garden of Eden she'd ever seen.

A long, high-pitched whistle, reminiscent of a

catcall, filled the air around her, defiling the sanctified area. She'd been so absorbed in the nature around her, she hadn't thought to be on the alert for others, people who had something to hide in these woods. Another whistle, and it seemed to have gotten closer. Now she heard men's voices—two or three? No, four. Prickles of unadulterated fear washed over her arms.

"Hey, now there's a bunny hole I'd like to hop in. Heh-heh."

"Come here, Bambi! Come to Papa!"

"Hey, little birdy, tweet your ass over here. I got my own birdy for ya!"

"She sure looks good enough to eat. There's enough for all of us to get a piece."

Damn it! Damn it! Damn it! This is not good. Not good at all. Where the hell do I go? I can't see any goddamn one of them! She crouched down by the nearest bush to catch her breath and muster her wits. If she couldn't see them, how were they able to see her? Did they have her surrounded? The only way to find out was to start moving toward camp and look sharp. If she didn't say anything and ignored them, maybe they'd give up and try their sick stalker game on someone else.

She slithered on the ground like the worms she'd photographed earlier.

"I'm gonna slide right up in ya, sugar. What do ya say?"

She gasped and shrieked as the voice and a body dropped onto her from above. God bless her jeans, because they were the only thing separating his hard-on from doing exactly what he threatened. "Uhhh." As most of the air left her body, her mouth watered, thirsting for a quick replacement. But the man's heavy body refused to yield, until another man voice yelled at him and pulled him off.

"Jesus, Josiah! You're gonna kill her before we've had our fun, you dumb shit!" She coughed and gasped for a much-needed breath, and, when she flipped over, she found two men grappling with each other on the ground. Taking advantage of the distraction, she scrambled to her feet and ran like a fleeing gazelle.

"Fuck you, Ezrah! I found her for us. I get first dibs."

"You ain't gonna have no piece of her, idiot. Look! She's running away."

Those were the last words she heard from the pair, and she wondered where the other two were. No sooner had she thought it than two scraggly-looking men with long, stringy hair and dirty clothes dropped from the trees. They had her caught between the camper and the other two thugs she hoped she'd left behind. One signaled to the other to spread their coverage so she had nowhere to run.

"Where do you think you're going? We're not done with you yet."

"Nope, the party's just begun. You're a bit overdressed for the occasion. Let's see if we can do something about that."

Frozen, she didn't know where to turn. Even climbing a tree wouldn't help her. All she envisioned was a cruel, violent sexual assault and possible death. "Please, I don't want any trouble. I want to go home to my family."

"Did ya hear, Kane? She wants to go home. Ain't that sweet?" Ezrah giggled, pretending to be a schoolgirl, then spat on the ground near her feet. "We'll take ya home, all right. You're coming with us. You got yourself a new home and family now. Jeremiah, help me and the others gather the bitch up, please."

"No!" The two stalked toward her, and everywhere she turned to try and escape, one of the

48

four was there, corralling her for the imminent takedown.

She screamed bloody hell and struck out at whatever came near her. She knew no one of consequence would hear, but it was a reflex and her last-ditch effort. "Leave me alone! Help! Someone help me!"

They moved in until they were close enough for their musky, musty stench to offend her nose, and then four sets of hands grabbed at her, pulling her down to secure her. She lashed out with her feet and nails, hoping to cause severe enough damage they'd let her go. Her heel made contact with someone's balls, which bought her a hard smack to the cheek for her efforts. She gouged another's face with her nails, earning her a punch right to the eye. She saw stars, and the world swam about her for a few moments. Wailing until her voice gave way, she had nothing left in her to fight them off. Finally, they tied her up, hands behind her back. Anklebones ground against each other under the heavy rope securing them together, and her pulse raced at her wrists.

"Please don't do this," she croaked. "Please don't do this. Please don't do this." *Oh God, I'm a dead woman.*

Ezrah and Jeremiah, the tallest of the four, hoisted her up onto Josiah's shoulders, like a human scarf.

"How far to the truck?"

"'Bout a fifteen-minute walk. Can you handle it with her on your shoulders?"

"Don't have much choice since you put her on me, now do I?"

"Don't be a smartass. I was just asking a question."

She growled and whipped herself about, trying to do anything she could to keep from being taken. "Son of a bitch!" Josiah whacked her hard on the stomach.

"Uh...."

"Knock it off! Damn, you'd think she was one of our kind."

"Yeah, but she sure don't smell like it."

"The way she wrecked your face and Jeremiah's balls, she might as well be."

"Just what do you all suppose you're doing with that woman?" She couldn't see where the new voice had come from, but she took the opportunity of a newcomer on the scene to raise holy hell.

"Help me! Please! They're trying to kidnap me! I don't know them! Help me!"

"Shut the fuck up, you little bitch!" Josiah thumped her on the head. "Well, well, well. Lookie here, fellas. If it ain't the runt of the Tao pack come for more abuse. You sure are a glutton for punishment, ain't ya?"

"You call our little go-round a punishment? That was child's play. Shame you can't handle me on your own and gotta use the pack to try and damage me. Guess you don't have what it takes to really bring me down."

"Oh, killin' you is gonna be the highlight of my day, you punk-ass bastard."

The guy's voice sounded vaguely familiar, but she couldn't quite place it. "Help me, please! My name's Willow Bisset. I'm from California and I'm here on vacation."

"Don't believe a word she says. She's our sister and a pathetic liar."

"Don't you mean pathological, you dumbass?"

"Whatever. You best go on and let us get on with our business. We'll be coming for you next. Take a last run of the land before you're good and dead."

"You see, now, I don't think I can do that. I'm gonna ask you to put her down gently and be on your way. We can catch up later, if you know what I

51

mean."

"Get the fuck outta here, man! We ain't leavin' her. She's ours. Jeremiah, Kane, finish off this asshole." Josiah hefted her on his shoulder again and started walking away. A low, rumbling growl made him stop in his tracks. "Nice teeth you got there. You know we got some, too. Wanna see?"

He leaned over to his right and let go of her. Slammed to the ground, she yelped and hoped she hadn't broken any ribs. He kicked her and said, "Stay the fuck put or else." Finally able to see the noble stranger, she was glad to be on the ground already, because, otherwise, she would have fallen from the shock. Greyson. Wherever the hell he'd come from, she blessed his return and wriggled out of the way. Josiah followed her and stepped on her ass.

"I said stay put," he snarled and released his foot, only to replace it with his grungy Wolf body.

"I...can't...breathe."

Along with a low grumble, the Wolf moved and stretched out across her legs.

She watched as Greyson shivered and shifted into the white Wolf, while the other three followed suit. Greyson stood taller, broader, more majestic than the others, and they were downright mangy. The power play fascinated her. They bared their teeth and snarled menacingly as they circled each other. One of the smaller gray Wolves leaped onto the haunches of Greyson first, and the melee ensued. Each of the smaller Wolves jumped on his back, bit him, and fell off, letting the next one do the same.

Greyson shook each attack off with little problem, but Willow could see the injuries from the other day hadn't quite healed yet. If these Wolves did more damage, he might not be able to recover. He went on the offensive, disregarding the other two's attacks while he zeroed in on one. Head low, teeth bared and intimidating, he leaped and clamped down on the one Wolf's throat. He raised his head and shook it, the Wolf still very much in his mouth. Blood spurted like a fountain and spotted his beautiful white coat. At least it wasn't his own blood, this time. With one strong shake, he tossed the lifeless assailant into the bushes.

He turned his attention to the next one, and the two retreated, heads low, tails tucked in. Josiah changed into a man, stood up, and jogged over to the others. They shifted to men, too, panting and sweating profusely.

Josiah turned to face Greyson and extended a

pointed finger toward him. "What you've done...we'll be looking for retribution. Don't bother sleeping ever again. Mark my words, your days and your pack's days are numbered. And we'll be back for her, too." The three ran over to their fallen comrade. Shifting into Wolf form, Josiah picked him up by the scruff. They ran off, howling their discontent.

The white Wolf limped over to Willow, sniffed her face, and licked her cheek. She laughed and cried, "Thank you." He nuzzled her neck and moved behind her. She felt his mouth and teeth on her hands. He gnawed on the rope binding her hands together until it frayed and she could pull them free. Her wrists were now graced with bright red chafing marks for bracelets, a souvenir, she thought mirthlessly, from her grand vacation. Sitting up and leaning over, she worked the ropes free from her ankles.

The white Wolf stood still before her. She scrabbled over to him, wrapped her trembling arms about his neck, and found comfort in the softness of his fur. She came undone as sobs and tremors racked her body.

From nestling fur, she found herself sitting in his lap, arms wrapped around his neck, her head snuggled in the crook of it. He set her on the ground before him. "You're safe now, Willow. I won't let them get near you ever again."

She looked up at him and dried her soaked cheeks with her shoulders. She sought answers in his eyes and found none, only unease and confusion. "Who are they? Who are *you*? Please, tell me."

"It's a long story. I promise I'll tell you, but, first, let's get you somewhere safe."

"My camper is a joke when it comes to safety."

"I had no intention of bringing you there. I have a cabin not too far away. We can get your camper and move it to my home."

"Or, I can pick up and get the hell outta Dodge." She tried to stand, but her legs were far too wobbly. "Shit, no sense leaving. I...I can't even stand up. What am I going to do?" She raked her hands through her tangled hair and shook her head, completely at a loss. This vacation had turned into a nightmare of vast proportions, and all she wanted to do was end it.

Without a moment's hesitation, Greyson picked her up and began walking. She wrapped her arms around his neck and closed her eyes, feeling safer than she'd ever felt in her life. With a sense of calm returning, she faded.

***

"We're here."

"Hmm?" Her eyes fluttered open and she yawned while looking around at familiar surroundings. "Wow! That was fast. What'd you do, run all the way?" She laughed.

"Walking takes too long. Do you think you can stand?"

"I don't know. Let me give it a try."

He lowered her legs and kept his arm around her waist. She tested the waters. No longer shaky, she took a couple of steps and gave him a thumbs up. "Wonderful! Let's get going."

In under half an hour, she was behind the wheel and following Greyson's directions to his cabin. At points, she didn't think her truck or the camper would make it through the narrow, dirt path he called a road. But it wasn't long before she drove up to a modest log cabin in the middle of fucking nowhere.

She turned off the engine and faced him. "Not much for neighbors?"

"I like my privacy. Go get your essentials and the first aid kit."

"Sure." She flashed a quick smile, to combat his

stormy mood, and winced. Her left cheek and eye ached. "Oh man. I'm afraid to know what this is going to look like in the morning."

***

A foul mood had taken up residence in Greyson's body. The stitches on his stomach pulled as his wounds healed, and his right thigh felt like a hot griddle had been permanently pressed against it. He shouldn't have run with Willow in his arms, but he wanted to get her out of harm's way as quickly as possible. At the thought of what could have happened had he not been on his way to her and heard her screaming, his mood sank from foul to abominable.

He had no idea if there was something or someone in charge of this group of angry thugs to blame for his current condition and hers. Whoever they were, they obviously had him marked for a while. If he remembered correctly, and he was sure he did, they were the same ones who'd harassed him at Gee's bar not too long ago. No surprise then they'd shown up in the woods for another confrontation. They'd surprised him as he'd walked up his porch steps the other evening, and attacked before he could properly shift, getting in some brutal slashes and shredding his new shirt and jeans. He wasn't sure what pissed him off more: being taken by surprise or having to throw out new clothes.

Chasing down and kidnapping an innocent woman was below the belt and compromised the safety of all shifters living in the Black Hills. Not only did he have a rogue to dispatch, but now he had an unknown pack of Wolves with a hard-on for vengeance to get rid of, too. Drew didn't tolerate bullies in the pack—not even if they were newcomers seeking to come home. Whether they understood the rules or not, his assailants had marked themselves.

He'd have to play it real close to the vest with Willow and tell her only what she needed to know. She'd need the kind of protection only he could provide. He had no choice but to come clean when today left no doubt he was a Wolf. Major problems came along with that. He'd be in deep shit if the pack found out about her. They weren't mated. Ryker, the Enforcer, would have his ass for dinner after reading him the riot act about secrecy and preservation of the pack. If Greyson could emphasize how she saved him and he saved her, Ryker's response would likely not be so harsh. After all, his mate, Saja, was human.

He had one thing in his favor. No one knew where he lived, since he'd moved out so long ago and never invited anyone to his house. Protecting Willow from these angry men and his own pack would be an intricate juggling of plates.

So why bother?

Why the hell did he decide to go back to her? It could have been those Guinness-brown eyes of hers that blessed him as he awakened from the brutal assault. Or it could have been the way the fire glinted red off her long, wavy hair as she leaned over to ease him down to rest. Yes, it was both of those things, and more. He'd returned because he'd acted like a schmuck, and all she had done was save his sorry ass. She deserved better. At the very least an apology for calling her batshit crazy.

There was more to it, though. As much as he wanted to fight it, he was drawn to her. He'd never thought about relationships before. Who'd want a white-haired, pale-skinned gargantuan man as a mate? When he awoke at her camp and peered deep into her eyes, he found his soul's reflection. In an instant, their two souls had recognized each other and formed a bond he wasn't so sure could ever be broken. Not even with his leaving her. He wondered

59

if she'd experienced the same thing as he, and, at the same time, didn't want to risk knowing the truth of it.

Why me, damn it? Why me?

"Here's the first aid kit and my suitcase." Willow closed the front door behind her and sat down on a wooden rocking chair by the woodstove. She leaned back and closed her eyes. That woman was lucky to be alive right now. But her face seemed pained, and the swelling wasn't going to improve unless he did something about it. He staggered over to the refrigerator, took out an ice pack, wrapped it in a paper towel, and brought it to her.

"Put this on your cheek and eye for a bit. It should keep the swelling down."

Without opening her eyes, she reached out a hand and fished around until she connected with the pack. "Thank you."

He rummaged through the kit. "Hey, you got anything in here for pain?"

"All I have are the usual suspects, acetaminophen, ibuprofen. Take your pick."

"Aaaah! They won't do. I guess I'll get another ice pack for myself."

"We're a hot mess."

"But we're alive. Thanks to you," he called from

the kitchen.

"And you!"

He hobbled back into the living room holding the ice pack on his right thigh. "Here, let me take a look at that eye of yours."

Standing beside her, he peeled her hand and ice pack away from her cheek. "I'm gonna get those bastards and make them pay."

"That bad, huh?"

"Well, I see a cut I didn't notice before. Right under your eye." He reached into the first aid kit and dug out the antibiotic ointment, some gauze, and tape. Kneeling, he turned her face toward him so he could fix her. "Here, let me put some of this stuff on."

"What a difference a day makes, huh? I mean, yesterday, I was playing nurse to you. Today...." She rested a cold, clammy hand on his arm before he could tend to her wound. "I honestly think I would have died today if you hadn't been there to save me." She released him and swiped a tear away from her good eye.

He dabbed the ointment gently on the cut and noticed more tears falling than she could wipe away at one time. He backed off, not sure what to do about it. It seemed as though he should comfort her, but what did he know of comfort? No one had ever consoled him, save for Betty a time or two. What had she done? She'd patted his shoulder and told him everything would be all right. So, he figured, it couldn't hurt to try. He reached out and patted her on the arm a couple of times and told her everything would be all right, but that only brought on stronger tears.

Now what the hell did he do? *Walk away. Just walk away and let her deal.* He returned to the kitchen and leaned against the sink, shoulders slumped at his ineptitude in handling a crying girl. He could fix a cut or a scrape. Emotional wounds stymied him.

She shuffled into the kitchen, sniffling and wiping her eyes and nose with a strip of toilet paper. Leaning up against the counter next to him, she nudged his arm. "Next time someone falls apart in front of you, a hug works very well."

"Sorry." He offered a weak smile. "I don't hang around people too much. It's better that way."

"Why?"

"Look at me."

"Yeah, so?"

He shrugged. "I'm...different, and it makes

people uncomfortable. So, I stay away."

"Greyson, the more you hang around people, the more normalized they become to anything you have to offer. Believe it or not, your look is something male models seek out. It's very unique and exotic."

"I'm an oddity, not exotic. Are you feeling better? Can I bandage your wound?"

She smirked. "Changing the subject, are we? I'll let it go, for now. And, yes, you may patch me up. Then, I need to have a look at you."

"All right, back into the living room."

"Or shall we rename it Greyson General Hospital?"

Chapter Four

"Take off your shirt and pants so I can check you out."

Greyson's eyebrows raised and he smirked. "Sure."

"Boy, that did not come out the way I planned!" She blanched and paid much interest to the first aid kit on the floor by the rocking chair. "Um, when you're done, sit on the floor so I can check out your back. Lord knows what damage those guys did to you today."

He grunted and when she lifted her gaze, he was naked as a jaybird sitting on the floor.

"Jesus Christ!" She twirled around and looked straight at the grandfather clock by the stairs. "Where the hell's your underwear?"

"I forgot, I guess. Being a Wolf half the time, well—"

"Holy...okay, then grab a pillow, would you?"

"Okay, you can turn around."

"Thank you." She couldn't hide the flush creeping in to replace her shock. She'd seen enough to know his size matched his size! "All right, let me take a look at you." She knelt behind him and seethed. "Damn. They did a number on you. Hand me the hydrogen peroxide and some cotton balls. We have to wash these out, and I'll butterfly tape them."

"What's it look like?"

"Oh, you've got a back full of connect the puncture wounds all over."

"Don't worry too much. They'll be gone by tomorrow, probably. I'll let my Wolf out and they'll heal up fine."

"Speaking of Wolf, you promised me some answers. I've got a lot of work here, so you might as well start sharing."

"What do you want to know?"

"You *know* what. Who were those beasts out there? What *are* you? What the *hell* have I stumbled into here?"

"They are like me. As you saw, we are Wolves as well as men. We can shift in and out of our Wolf selves. Some do it according to the moon. Others of us can do it whenever we want. I have no idea who these guys are beyond their names. Somehow, I seem to have pissed them off enough to trek here from wherever they live and make sure *I* don't live for very much longer. For all I know, it could be related to my job. Who knows?"

"Sounds like you have a dangerous job."

"Someone's gotta do it. Dangerous Wolves need to be handled to keep the rest safe. I got a knack for tracking, so it's what I do."

"And once you've found the bad Wolves, then what?"

"Well, then things get ugly for them and they die."

"I see." His matter-of-fact response unnerved her, but this wasn't her world, and she had no right to judge. "How is it that you can shift? How did you all become—"

"Wolves? You can say it. That's what we are. I don't know. All I know is I was born and left to die right here in these woods by a mother who didn't want a runt."

"That's horrible and tragically sad. And you're no runt! You're larger and stronger than those other Wolves."

"But I'm different from all the others. I was adopted by a man, a shifter, too, and he raised me. There are those of us on this earth who are different from humans. We don't like attention, don't want it, and keep our existence a closely guarded secret."

"So, now that I know, are you gonna have to kill me?"

He said nothing.

She froze mid-dab.

"I won't ever hurt you. But there are those in the pack who would hurt us both if they found out about you without knowing the whole story. I'm here to make sure it doesn't happen."

"Wow, thanks for your honesty. I don't know whether to be totally freaked out or relieved." She continued to wash down his wounds. "What if I left? Just pretend this all never happened? I could go to so many other places to camp out—"

"Until those jerks who grabbed you today and anyone else they told about you are caught and dealt with, you'll never be safe, wherever you go. They have your scent and they will find you."

"Shit." She slumped on her ass. *What a fucking mess!* She gave herself a moment to gather herself together, then put on a brave front.

"Sorry, but I didn't think you should go around thinking everything is fine and dandy. That could kill you."

"I appreciate it. Lie down so I can check your stomach. Those gashes were all sorts of nasty the other day."

He lay flat on the floor, and his eight-pack rippled into spectacular shape. She had to catch herself from sighing aloud. His body was one of pure perfection and as white as fresh-fallen snow. When she peeled back the gauze protecting the cuts, the edges of the sewn-up slashes didn't seem as fierce and fiery red as the day before.

"These are ready to come out. How is this possible?" she murmured.

"After I left, I shifted into my Wolf. We heal faster that way. I told you I'd be fine in a couple of days."

"So you did. Then you left." She couldn't keep the hurt out of her voice, and she was angry with herself for letting him know how he'd hurt her. She took surgical scissors from the box and cut the stitches away. Then she put more ointment on them and covered them up.

"I'm sorry. I thought it was best for us both. And

I'm sorry for calling you crazy."

"I need to check your thigh now." Nope, she wasn't going to give in so easily and accept his apology. She crawled over to his right side and paused. "This is going to sound terrible, but I need you to spread your legs so I can get in there and change the dressing."

He said nothing but pasted a wicked grin on his face. She had to look away or she'd get lost in his smoldering eyes. This would not end well if she were to get distracted by him. He shifted his legs apart, and she crept between them. The injury started at the top of his thigh and traveled down and inward toward his groin.

As she peeled back the tape, he jerked. "Just rip the damn thing off, okay?"

"All right." She cringed and tore it away.

"Yow!" He sat up and let go of the pillow protecting his manhood from curious eyes. "That hurt worse than the wound itself does!"

She covered her face, trying to control her laughter as he lay back down. "I know it's not funny, but it's funny! I'm sorry. I'll stop." She looked down to continue her observation and redressing. "Oh my God! Cover up!" Her blush returned with a vengeance.

"You've seen me already. Why bother?" He took the pillow and propped his head with it.

She couldn't speak or think of a witty retort, so she took a deep breath and focused on the gnashed muscle. It, too, had healed remarkably well, but it still needed a cleaning and change of dressing. The muscular tissue seemed to have regrown since she first tended to it. Astounding.

She dabbed the cotton ball, soaked with the antiseptic, on the raw flesh. His penis flinched with each pass of the cleanser. *Dear Lord in Heaven, give me strength not to lean my head down!* She spread the antibiotic ointment on next, and his penis hardened against the back of her hand. She froze and stopped breathing. *Why do you test me, Lord? Why?* She took in a shallow breath and layered gauze onto the wounded area and taped it up. When she leaned back to sit on her heels, she placed her hands in her lap. He sat up and took her chin in his hand. His blue and gold eyes speared straight to her heart and soul and spoke of trust, faith, and loyalty.

"Thank you." He leaned in, closed his eyes, and placed a gentle, tremulous kiss upon her lips. He lingered, tasting more and more of her, and she? She fell fast into a whirlpool of emotions. *What should I do? Where are we going with this? The man is sitting naked, inches away from me! The man is a Wolf.*

He pulled away and then rested his forehead against hers. "Next time a man kisses you, you should try kissing him back, and maybe put your arms around his neck and pull him toward you. Let him know you want him."

She licked her lips and nibbled on the bottom one. *Touché, Mr. Wolf.*

"Willow, don't think about what I am. It's only half of me. You saved the man the other day. It's the man sitting before you now, and the man who kissed you, hoping you'd want to kiss him, too." His voice, hoarse with emotion, dropped down to but a whisper. "Kiss me, Willow, please."

A tear dared to fall on her cheek at his plea, and her heart hurt so, she felt as though it had been roasted over a raging fire. She cupped his face in her hands, gazed into his eyes, and found her soul within them. Tipping her head, she bridged the distance between them and laid her lips against his. His mouth opened slightly, and she followed his cue. When his tongue touched hers, she mewled, and

71

explored the warmth within. He wrapped his arms about her waist and pulled her so close, the heat and tension of his body enveloped her.

His hands blazed a scorching trail under her shirt to knead her shoulder blades then down her pants to cup her ass. She tore her lips from his and groaned. "Greyson...."

"Hmm?" He feathered kisses along her jaw to her throat and lingered, licking and lightly sucking.

"You're naked." She ran her fingers through his thick mane as he nipped at her earlobe.

"Mm-hmm." He moved on to her collarbone and shoulder as he pushed aside her T-shirt and bra strap.

"Ooh. Mmm...I'm not."

"I can help you with that." In one swift motion, he grabbed the hem of her shirt and pulled it clean off without so much as touching her bad cheek and eye. Then he leaned forward and nestled his lips in the swells of her breasts as he released her bra. He took a moment to draw each one into his mouth to suck and tease with his tongue. His hot breath sent waves of shivers up her spine and butterflies down low. He raised up on his hands and knees, and, with his mouth against her belly, pushed her to lie down.

Tracing a path to the waistline of her jeans, he unbuttoned them with his teeth. He grabbed the zipper, too, and pulled. She marveled at his ability. Using his hands, he tugged the jeans and her panties down, continuing to feather kisses where heat had built up and she'd gone damp with need and raging desire.

Willow's hands shook as she reached out to touch him, but he was too far away, kissing, licking, and sucking, nipping and thrusting his tongue inside her, whipping her into a frenzy of mind-blowing sexual sensation. He'd hooked his arms under her thighs, so there was nowhere to escape from his attentions, and she bucked and ground against him. She grabbed fistfuls of his hair until she cried out, "Oh God! Greyson! Ah! No more, no more, no more!"

He kissed her inner thighs and every inch of her on his lazy way up her body, still racked with spasms, and, when his face was even with hers, he kissed her hard on the mouth. She tasted herself on him and it stoked the flames even higher. She needed him inside her. To be one with him. Her soul would not rest until they did so.

"Greyson, I need you. Inside me, Greyson. I need. I need." She grabbed his ass and pulled him to her as she spread her legs apart.

"Whoa, whoa, wait a second. Wait a second. We're gonna do this right." He disentangled himself from her and, as he stood, he collected her in his arms to take the stairs three at a time. What the hell was she doing? Before she could grapple with her momentary lapse of reason, he laid her upon his king-size bed, went to the bathroom, and returned with a strip of condoms. He tore a packet off, and hurriedly rolled one on. "Okay, now where were we?' He eased himself down, but not enough to crush her, and the heat between them could have started a real fire. "Oh, right. Here."

He nudged his penis against her clit and rubbed, sending her soaring to delirious oblivion. He entered her slowly and pulled out even slower. Knowing how large he was, it amazed her how well he fit inside. Thrusting in and out, again and again, he picked up the pace. Willow had never experienced sex like this before. She thought she'd had orgasms, thought she'd been loved up right, but Greyson had proved her very wrong.

It felt good to be wrong.

Grabbing her ass, he held her strong, thrusting deep and hard. With every push, her heart came more and more undone, and she cried out her ecstasy. Maneuvering her onto her stomach, he hooked a leg in the crook of his arm and opened her up. Grunting and groaning above her, he leaned in, kissing the base of her spine and licking and nipping his way up to her neck. She could tell he was close to coming as his thrusts became erratic and frenzied. His whole body seized, and he clamped down on the fleshy part at the base of her throat as he climaxed. She screamed out his name as she followed him to the promised land. In those final moments, she felt something tug at the very fabric of her being. Something so innocent, so true, so essential to life itself. Deep within, Greyson laid claim. His essence suffused her mind, body, and soul, and she knew in that instant, she was his and he was hers.

After slowly pulling out, he fell to the side to rest on his stomach. As she turned to lie on her back, he grabbed her to him and draped his arm protectively over her stomach and chest. Panting, his skin dewy with sweat, he looked over at her and smiled. With her fingers, she stroked his cheek, soft and stubble-free, and returned the smile.

"Greyson, I felt something as we made love."

"Me, too. Me, too."

"No, silly. I mean something other than an orgasm."

He turned on his side and raised up on an elbow to prop his head. "Okay, what did you feel?"

"I'm not sure I can even explain it properly, and I don't want to freak you out by appearing possessive or anything, but when I look at you now, all I think is...*mine*. Like in a cavewoman type of way, you know? It's crazy! I don't know. Forget I said anything." She grabbed a pillow and covered her head, completely embarrassed.

He pulled it away and offered her a genuine smile. "You don't sound crazy. I felt it, too. It's never happened to me before, and I'll admit to having sex a time or two. I didn't expect this to happen between us. I'm sorry I bit you. I hope it doesn't hurt."

"No, I kinda liked it, actually."

"I don't want to alarm you, either, but there's a reason you and I are feeling the way we do."

"Why would I be alarmed? We just had the most incredible sex I've ever known!"

He caressed her cheek. "I believe we've mated."

"Mated?" She scoffed.

He nodded.

"As in, you and I are stuck with each other for

life, mated?"

He nodded again.

Her mind was officially blown.

"Which brings with it a host of issues I don't want to think about right now." He scrubbed his face with his hands and then looked up at the ceiling. "On a scale of one to ten, how pissed are you?"

"One to ten? Hmmm. I want to say a hundred."

"Shit," he muttered.

"But I can't."

"Hmm?" He turned a confused face to her.

She sat up and tried to put into words all the emotions coursing through her. "I should be royally pissed right now, but I can't be. You're...you're a part of me now, like the very blood running through my veins. The air I breathe. To deny our bond would be to deny my own existence. Where I got these feelings from, I have no clue, but I believe it. Crazy."

"Shit, that's mated talk if I ever heard it. This is going to be difficult. If we come out of this with our lives, we'll be the luckiest people on the planet."

"You're afraid. Funny how you'd think the *human* here would be the one tucking tail and running from this fate. If you don't want this, tell me now, and we'll find a way to reverse it."

"There is no reversing it, and I didn't say I didn't want it. I'm worried about the consequences. You don't know my pack or its rules. We have to tread carefully for this to work, but I swear on my life, I won't let anything happen to you."

She slid down and rested her head in the crook of his arm. "I believe you. And I will do the same." She needed to move on to a different topic or she'd fall to pieces. Her life had been irreparably changed and the implications known and unknown were too much to handle at the moment. So, she placed those sticky morsels in a tidy little box and set it aside to be dealt with later. "Say, I saw you bring a whole string of condoms from the bathroom."

"Yes."

"I'm up for the challenge if you are." She wiggled her eyebrows and sucked on her index finger. His penis twitched and hit her upper thigh.

"A challenge where we both win? I'm in." He kissed her hand as she teased his lips with the same finger. "But first, your eye and cheek need some icing down. Stay put. I'll get the packs."

"Come to think of it, they do hurt like a son of a bitch. Thanks for the lovely distraction, though. Sex really is a painkiller." As he reached the bedroom door, she stopped him. "Hey, do you have any food? I could eat a bear right now."

"Good thing Gee's not here to hear your remark." He laughed.

"Who's Gee? Or should I ask *what*?" She raised a brow.

"The man who adopted me. He's a bear shifter."

"Well, that's downright terrifying."

"Oh, he's a teddy bear most of the time. Just don't get on his bad side."

"Seeing as though I'm human, I think the 'bad side' is my middle name."

"I've got a bag of chips and a jar of dip. Okay?"

"Perfect. I'll be here eagerly awaiting."

He stalked over to the bed and pounced on top of her. She shrieked and giggled as he munched on her neck and whispered in her ear what he'd rather eat. Then, he abruptly fled the room and returned a few minutes later. Her second orgasm came when he put the ice pack on her face. That might have been an exaggeration, but it felt so damn good. They polished off the bag of chips in under ten minutes.

"I think our challenge will have to wait. We need to heal well and completely, Willow, so keep the ice pack on your face. You heal with ice and pills. I have my way. I have to shift. I want you to know so you don't freak out."

"Thank you. I'm ready." She held the ice to her face and watched as he shivered and turned. It appeared like a wave of fur overtaking his body from his head down to his toes, or paws. He shook out his fur and lay down alongside her, but on top of the covers. He rested his muzzle against her shoulder, licked it a couple of times, and then closed his eyes. She closed hers, too, as the cool pack soothed her aching face.

**

Although they'd gone to sleep far too early, they both slept through until morning. She awoke first and turned on her side to watch the white Wolf sleep. How strange her reality had become. If someone were to have told her creatures existed who shifted into men and women, she'd have thought them crazy. Yet, here she was, in bed with a beautiful Wolf who would become a man in a matter of seconds.

A snuffle and a yawn, and that's exactly what happened. In a matter of moments, Greyson appeared, naked and lying on top of the covers. Without a word, he collected her into his arms, and she melted against his body that thrummed with latent power.

"Good morning, sweetness." He lightly stroked the locks of hair that had fallen to his chest.

"Mmm, good morning."

"How did you sleep?"

"Like the dead. I only woke up a few minutes ago."

"Good. Your eye looks like shit."

"Gee, thanks." She slapped playfully at his chest. "It doesn't throb like it did yesterday."

He released her and hopped out of bed. "I'll get you some pills and a fresh ice pack. Don't go anywhere."

"Well, I gotta pee. But I promise I'll be waiting in bed as long as you'll join me. You know, we still have the whole strip to go through."

"Deal."

***

The wounds on Greyson's back had healed completely and left no trace, while the ones on his stomach were almost gone. His thigh, on the other hand, still needed a bit more time. They spent the whole day in bed or in the kitchen or the living room.

In fact, there wasn't a room or surface they hadn't used in some way shape, or form to make love. Willow's favorite so far was the shower, and she put in a special request for another few go-rounds in there before the day was done.

Chapter Five

The white Wolf had the rogue in his sights. After two weeks of playing cat and mouse, he'd finally caught him unawares. Could have been there was no breeze to carry his scent. It was downright muggy, and he could almost drink the air, it was so thick with humidity. The red Wolf was lapping up water by a stream. His fur seemed matted and stained with dried blood, a good sign he'd be an easy catch and kill. With Greyson's thigh still a bit tender, he was grateful the rogue was injured, too.

He wondered, though, what had attacked the Wolf. Another Wolf? A bear? It didn't really matter. He'd be the one to bring him down in the end. Step by painstaking step, he approached from the rear, while the target remained fixated on quenching his thirst. It was all textbook now. Greyson was close enough and pounced on the other's back. Snarls and barks filled the air, and the battered Wolf tried in vain to shake him off. In a matter of moments, he finished him off with a jaw-widening bite to the throat.

Once the Wolf's body hung limp in his grip, he released him. With Wolves shifting differently, he waited to see if this one would turn or stay Wolf. He didn't turn, so he was moon dependent. The Tao Pack had one less rogue Wolf to worry about. He picked up the body and ran it all the way to Los Lobos, where he left it at Ryker's doorstep. Shifting to his human form, he pulled a note out of his jeans pocket and shoved it in the dead Wolf's mouth.

One rogue Wolf tracked and killed, as per instructions. The Tao Pack can rest easier tonight.

He pulled the hood of his long-sleeved shirt over his head and trudged over to Gee's Bar to wash up and have a quick lunch. It was hot as hell, but it beat getting stared at by curious eyes. He sat at his regular spot at the bar counter and ordered up lunch from Paul, the waiter.

"Two times in two weeks I see you here."

Gee's familiar voice and cadence raised a smile on his face. "I missed your ugly mug." He swiveled around on the stool to see the Werebear putting on his apron.

"You need help or food?"

"A bit of both, actually, if you could spare some time. I need to run something past you." Paul brought over three hamburgers and two orders of fried pickles.

"Eat first, then we talk." Greyson scarfed down his meal in no time and stood at the door of his office. "Sit."

He fell into a worn recliner and pulled down his hood. "I'm not sure where to begin."

"At the beginning is best."

"I wasn't looking for it. It just happened. And now, I have all these feelings running through me I gotta get a handle on. I...I—"

"What *is* it?"

"I've mated." He pushed the hood up over his head and leaned his elbows against his knees. "Don't tell anyone, all right? I'm telling you because I gotta tell someone, and I trust you. It's complicated."

Gee grunted and leaned as far as his rickety office chair would go.

"What's there to be complicated about? You found a girl. You had sex. You found your mate. So

85

who is it?"

"None of the girls from Tao."

"Then from which pack?"

"None."

"I see."

"Do you? Do you really?"

Gee leaned forward and moved from his chair to the corner of his desk, right in front of him.

"Grey, you are not one of us by blood. Since your birth, you've never had it easy. It seems fate has decided you should live a complicated life. So, I am assuming the worse-case scenario. I smell human on you. I'm thinking you mated with a human woman. Am I right?"

He nodded and hung his head.

"Then be proud and courageous about it! You will have to defend your mating to Drew and Ryker. You show weakness and doubt about your commitment to her and this pack, and you can kiss your life and your woman's good-bye. Show you will lay down your life for her, and she you, and you will be fine. Will she be trouble for us?"

"I haven't spoken to her about it yet. She only found out I'm a Wolf the other day. I did tell her we needed to tread carefully. I told her how secretive we need to be to protect the pack, but I need her to know, beyond a shadow of a doubt, that her life and mine are in jeopardy if she should ever expose us."

"You must do this as soon as possible. How do you know you can trust her otherwise?"

"I don't. But I can feel it, sense it. She'd never betray us. Never."

"I will keep this secret for now, my son. You need to sort this out quickly before fate takes another turn."

He nodded, stood, and shook Gee's hand. "Thank you."

Next on his to-do list? Find the three assholes who'd hurt Willow and wanted him dead. He'd kill them all. One by one if necessary. Slowly and painfully, too, if the mood struck him. No one threatened his life and the lives of his pack and mate without consequences. He normally wasn't one for sadistic pleasure, but he would make an exception this time.

***

Willow may have been on vacation, but Greyson was not. He had a job to do, which he did not elaborate on, and had to leave her alone in his house. He didn't appear too happy about it, and made it clear she was not to leave or make it appear as though anyone lived there. He said he'd be home before dark and there was food in the pantry and refrigerator. He kissed her long and hard, and his hungry eyes told her he'd be having her for dinner.

Just thinking about their exchange made her hot and her pulse race. This whole mating thing boggled her mind. Ever since they'd made love, no...ever since she'd cared for him, he was all she could think about, all she wanted to breathe in and touch and taste and hear. His very existence monopolized her world. But his going off to do his job forced her to think about her own career once again.

She hadn't taken any pictures since being assaulted and kidnapped. But did she really need to anymore? She had those pictures of him shifting from Wolf to man. She'd be a star when they went public. And yet, something disturbing lingered in the recesses of her mind. Greyson alluded to some pretty ominous consequences for their mating, and he'd mentioned about how crucial secrecy was to his pack.

This was a fine conundrum she found herself in. To publish or not to publish, that was the question.

Whether to delete them and return to a job she hated with every fiber of her being, or expose him to the world and never have to worry about another job ever again. What kind of life would she have with him if she revealed his true identity? What could happen if people questioned the existence of more like him? His pack could be compromised. His own life could be turned into a series of scientific experiments, or he could be seen as a freak-show circus attraction. He'd never forgive her. If his pack didn't kill her, he surely would. And she wouldn't blame him.

No, it wouldn't do at all. It wasn't for her to reveal anything about what she'd seen. Now that she was his mate, his pack's safety naturally became her responsibility. She needed to delete those pictures and come clean about it to him. He didn't even know she was a photographer to begin with. In all honesty, he didn't know jack shit about her, and neither she about him, other than he was a werewolf. As hefty a nugget of information as it was, it certainly wasn't enough. When he got home, they needed to get to know each other well beyond the physical. If they were mated, they needed to know everything about each other.

First, she needed to get her camera and SD card.

Then she could delete the pictures and take some new ones of the humming birds she noticed right outside the kitchen window. Not nearly as impressive, but less inflammatory. She threw on a pair of shorts and a T-shirt and tiptoed down the stairs. She laughed when she realized what she'd done. Slowly, she opened the front door and peered out in all directions. Greyson wouldn't be happy with her, but she was going stir-crazy anyway and needed something to occupy her time while he was gone.

The coast seemed clear, so she scurried over to her camper and grabbed her purse and camera bag. Just as quickly, she ran to the cabin and locked the door behind her as soon as she entered. She looked down at her hands, shaking furiously, and took deep breaths to calm herself. Dumping the bags on the couch, she tore upstairs to wash up and dress for real for the day.

His shower turned out to be divine. It had the perfect pressure to massage the aches away. She was careful to keep her cheek and eye away from the stream, but her back and shoulders were in desperate need of some attention. Dried and naked, she examined herself in the mirror. The cut by her eye had scabbed over and was surrounded by an island of black, blue, and yellow. It hadn't migrated to her nose or even down her cheek, so she considered herself lucky, especially with what she'd been through.

She scrutinized her face and her body. Did she look different now that she'd mated? Not really. Except for the bite mark, she appeared as she had days prior to their meeting. But if Greyson were to look into her eyes, and she into his, she bet they'd find each other there. She pulled her hair into a loose ponytail and dressed. Damn it! She missed him already, and he'd only been gone a couple of hours. It was going to be a long day.

***

The white Wolf returned to where the assault happened and sniffed, picking up the other Wolves' scents to track them to their den or human homes. He needed to find each one, alone, and, to do so, he'd need to use his wits. Their scent still lingered and trailed off to the east. He remembered, when he bit into the one, how filthy and disgusting he was. No wonder the scent still hung in the air.

The path wound through the forest, along streams and over waterfalls until he came across a run-down shack. He stopped and lay low for a while, watching and scoping out the place. All seemed quiet, but one never knew. It was around noon, so they could have been out foraging for food or even at a human job. He'd waited long enough. No one appeared to be home, so he trotted around the cabin and stood on his hind legs to peer through the window. He found the standard cabin items inside— chairs, couches, tables, beds. Nothing unusual or suspect.

There was one interesting item he noticed on a coffee table. There sat a picture collage of a mother and her four sons at different ages. One was when they were all babies. Quadruplets? Then as boys in their teens. They looked different from each other in this one. Curious. And the other two were again, the mother with her boys in their twenties and thirties. The men in the last picture were the four who tried to kidnap Willow. He figured to be around the same age as them.

He looked at the mother in all of the pictures, and something clicked. He had to go inside and get a closer look. He heard nothing alarming, saw nothing to worry about, so he shifted and tried the front door. It had been left unlocked. Once inside, he hustled over to the set of pictures and turned the frame over to remove them. He'd seen humans write on the backs of pictures to remind them of names and years. Maybe this mother did, too.

As he turned each one over, his hopes were confirmed. The earliest one, with the babies, was the last to be pried out. He took it and read the remarks.

"Should have been five boys, but there always has to be one runt in the litter. Ezrah, Josiah, Jeremiah, and Kane."

Holy shit. I think I just found my fucking family. And they wanted him dead. How's that for brotherly love? Who was he to talk? He wanted them dead now, too. This was all sorts of messed up. He sat dumbfounded on the floor by the coffee table, picture in hand, forgetting he was trespassing. He needed to get the hell out of there. If they came back and found him inside their home, there'd be a feast for dinner, and he'd be the one on the menu.

He slid the pictures into place and righted the frame on the table. Then he ran out of there, closed the door, and shifted, racing off at full speed to anywhere but there. He found his favorite spot, a cliff overlooking a waterfall, and collapsed. Howling at the top of his lungs, he didn't care who heard him. What kind of fucked-up life was this? Abandoned, left to die by his mother, now hunted like prey by his brothers. This was insane! And a kick to the gut. And psychological torture. He howled again, his heart hurting so much, he wanted to rip it out. Too much rejection can do serious damage to a person or a Wolf.

His anguish would not be abated, but the desire to find his brothers withered. He wanted to go home. He needed his mate. Yeah, he needed his mate, who accepted him for who and what he was. His mate, who he didn't know a thing about, but loved her to distraction anyway. This mating thing was crazy. But she would be able to soothe him. She'd be able to set his mind right again. She would love the rejection right out of him.

***

She needed a shave. She realized it after she showered. Back upstairs, she sat on the edge of the tub with shaver and cream in hand. In all the books and movies, werewolves were hairy, but hers had none save for his lashes, brows, and hair on his head. She would not present herself as hairier than he.

When he got home, he'd get a smooth woman.

With one last stroke to go, she heard someone come through the front door. "Greyson?" she called out.

"Yeah, it's me," he hollered. Then all went silent.

She grabbed a towel and dried off her legs.

"Hey, what's the meaning of this? Why is it here?"

She twisted around to find him in the doorway, a scowl on his face, holding her camera in the air accusingly.

"It's my camera." She reached out and tried to take it from him, but he yanked it out of reach. "Hey! I brought it over from the camper because I was bored and needed something to do. Can I have it, please?"

"Not yet. Why didn't you tell me you had a camera?"

"It never came up in any of our few conversations. Might I add, we've yet to have any conversation to get to know each other. I don't know the slightest thing about you save for being a Wolf shifter, and you know even less about me. Now, hand over my camera, Greyson. I'm a photographer. It's what I do for a living."

He lowered his hand and offered her the camera. The scowl remained.

"Thank you. Now, why don't we go downstairs and have a nice chat. I think we owe it to ourselves, don't you?"

He nodded, silently, and followed her down to the living room. She sat beside him, her heart racing at the thought of what she had to tell him. Given his current disposition, it probably wasn't going to go well at all. But she had no choice. She had to share everything, be open and honest, and then move on.

"You're sitting on my purse. Can I have it, please?"

"Oh, sorry." He lifted his butt and pulled it out, looking a bit embarrassed. "Here."

She took it and dug inside for the SD card. She prayed he was a good listener because he'd need to listen to everything very carefully.

"Willow, I came home, thinking the same thing as you. We don't know each other at all, and yet the mating called to us and brought us together despite that fact. So, tell me about you, and I'll tell you about me."

"Do you promise to listen to me and let everything I have to share with you sink in, without judgment?"

"Shit." He rubbed his hands on his knees. "This is going to be bad, isn't it?"

"Maybe, maybe not, but still."

"Yes, I will listen and not interrupt. Go ahead."

"I come from New York City. My parents were, are, strange, and raised my siblings and me in a very survival-of-the-fittest kind of way. Being a kid wasn't so bad, but any kind of warmth or loving emotions I have, I learned from my friends and their families. When each of us turned eighteen, they threw us out of the house and basically abandoned us to live their own lives free from familial entanglements. My brother and sister still live in New York but are such driven people, I haven't seen them more than a handful of times since they left. As for this thing...." She held up her camera. "I can't remember a time I didn't have a camera in my hands. I found my heart there and a way to express myself. The beauty missing from our home, I found in nature.

"Eventually, I turned my passion into a career. I photograph models for a magazine. It's not what I truly want to do, but it pays the bills. My passion still lies in nature photography." She paused, trying to gauge his reaction. So far, so good. "I came to this forest for a vacation and to reevaluate my life. I've decided to give up my fashion photography and make a go of it as a nature photographer. In order to do that, I have to find one moment, one event unique from all the others. A picture so astounding, it will write my ticket into the very difficult inner circle at *National Geographic.*"

"How has your picture-taking been going so far? Sorry, I forgot I wasn't supposed to interrupt."

She laughed. "That's okay. It *had* been going great. I have some amazing pictures of wondrous creatures in this forest. None are the 'money shot,' though. There's something I have to show you, but first I have to do something." She took the SD card from the baggie and exchanged it for the one already in her camera. Then, she turned it on and sorted through the pictures until she came to his. "Remember the night you were attacked?"

"Yes. What about it?"

"Well, you don't know this, but it happened right outside the campsite I was staying at. I brought you there to take care of you, with great effort I might add."

"For which I am so grateful."

"I heard the assault. It was horrible. All the

snarling, the growling, and yelping." She shook her head as her ears filled with auditory remembrances. "Before moving you, though, I was fascinated by your Wolf, so I grabbed my camera and took pictures, thinking what an incredible photo-essay I could create. And then you changed, right before my eyes. And I still took pictures."

He sat up straight, as if someone had put a rod in his spine. "Are you telling me you captured me shifting on camera?"

She looked down at the viewfinder and nodded. She passed it to him. "It was going to be my ticket to stardom, the launch of my career. But I want you to know, I'm deleting them. If you're interested in seeing exactly how you shift, go ahead and look. Greyson, the words you need to hear well and clear from me are *I'm deleting all the pictures.*"

He looked at the picture of the Wolf, and then he pressed the Play button for it to move to the next. He kept pressing until there were no more pictures to see. He sat back, a thunderstruck expression on his face. She couldn't tell if he was pissed, enthralled, or ready to kill. She retrieved the camera and pushed the Trash button and once again to delete the photos. She leaned in to him so he could see each picture as she deleted it, so there'd be no question about her loyalty.

"It's done."

He nodded.

"Are you going to say anything?"

"Are there any more?"

"No, those were the only ones."

"How do I know you're telling me the truth?"

Initially offended and ready to spew some snarky remark, she recoiled, realizing she'd have asked the same question if their positions were reversed. "I guess you have to believe me. You have to have faith in me. I didn't have to tell you at all, did I? I could've kept this all a secret, submitted the disk to *National Geographic*, and left this place, never to return again. But I didn't. Despite all the shit I've been through, I'm still here. Aren't I?"

"You're still here. And so is the camera. If anyone catches you with it, you're dead. I'm dead. You have to get rid of it."

"What? I can't do that!" Outrage shot through her like an arrow to the heart. "It's my livelihood! If this nature thing doesn't work out, I have to go back to my old job. I take pictures, Greyson. Telling me to get rid of this is like me telling you to give up your

Wolf. To never shift again."

"That's completely different."

"I beg to differ. The white Wolf is half of you. You can do things as a Wolf you couldn't do as a man. My camera is my eyes to the world, my mind's playing field, the vehicle for others to see my soul no matter how peaceful or disquieted it may be." Anger and fear mixed inside her. How could her mate ask such a thing of her? She jumped up from the couch, camera in hand. "You can't make me give it up. I can't. I won't!"

Running out the front door, she didn't care where her feet took her, as long as it was far from the cabin. Ironic. She should be running *toward* her mate and not away from him. Disappointment, anguish, and frustration were a heady combination. Her stomach roiled, and her head swam from it all.

"Willow! Come back here! Willow!" She heard footfalls behind her and gasped. Through waterlogged eyes, she'd run straight away from the house, wound up by a stream, and splashed through it to the other side. "Willow!"

Out of breath from crying and running at the same time, she tripped and fell over a hidden tree root. She managed to save the camera, sacrificing her elbows and knees instead. "Ah! Why? Why? Why did this have to happen to me? What did I do to deserve this?"

"Willow," an insistent voice, soft and low, purred her name. This voice seemed to be inside her head. Not out in the open.

"What? What?" She raised her arms in defeat.

"I'm sorry. I'm sorry about everything. I'm sorry you got hooked into this mating. I'm sorry you were assaulted. I'm sorry for not recognizing your feelings matter. I won't ever ask you to give up something important ever again. I promise. Come to me. Please. It's not safe out here."

She looked around to find the owner of the voice. The white Wolf stood a few yards away, submitting to her with his head hung low and tail between his legs. So, he could talk to her without speaking? Extraordinary! She swiped her eyes with the hem of her T-shirt, shook out her pine-needle-infested hair, and scrambled up from where she'd fallen. The mugginess of the day made all sorts of debris stick to her skin like she was one big, sticky lint roller. Holding her camera protectively, she stalked over to him, but he stepped away.

She sniffled as composure returned and frayed

nerves calmed. "I forgive you for being an insensitive oaf. Please forgive me for reacting like a spoiled brat rather than a rational woman defending her career."

He lowered his head in a nod and chuffed. "Now, stand tall, White Wolf, and walk with me to the cabin."

He rose to his full height and howled then nudged her free hand with his muzzle. She stroked his head and rested it on his back as they walked to his house in silence. When they arrived, he shifted into the man who'd so wrongly hurt her heart, and hoisted her up in his arms to carry her across the threshold.

"We're not married, you know."

"Might as well be. That was our first argument."

She slapped him playfully on his shoulder. "That means we get to have make-up sex."

"What's that?"

"Really, really good, hot sex."

"Oh, I like the sound of that." He sat down on the couch with her still in his arms.

"So, are we good here? I'm keeping my camera, and you're trusting I won't ever take a picture of you ever again."

"We're good. You can keep your camera. But it's

not just me you can't photograph. You can't photograph anyone from the pack or any other shifter."

She raised her hands in utter exasperation. "Well, how the hell am I supposed to know who is and who isn't a shifter?"

"I think it's safe to say if you must take nature pictures, you need to do it elsewhere. It's too risky here, Willow."

"That requires traveling. Are you willing to be without me for weeks on end?"

"That's not going to be possible. From what I hear, once mated, it's not pleasant to be apart for any length of time. We get antsy, irritable. I guess I'll have to join you on your trips."

"You would do that for me?"

"I'd do anything for you."

She blushed and caressed his cheeks as she looked upon his sweet, open face, then planted a tender kiss on his lips. "I'm a filthy mess. Come help me get clean, Greyson. We can play twenty questions to get to know each other, but you only get fifteen as compensation for making me cry."

"I don't know if we'll both fit in the tub, but I'm willing to try."

"Oh, it's deep enough, and anyway, you know how flexible I can be."

"Yes, yes I do."

Chapter Six

After showering off the grime of the forest, Greyson filled the tub with fresh, clean, hot water. He dipped a sponge and wrung it out over Willow's breasts peeking through the surface like icebergs.

"Mmm, more."

He did it again, then flipped her to swap places with him so she was fully submerged, and he took the brunt of the cool air.

"You're such a gentleman. One more thing I can add to the list I now know about you."

"Right after I make love to you again."

"Who am I to argue?"

She giggled, and, when his hardened shaft came a-knockin', playtime was over. She wrapped her legs around his waist as he entered her. For the second time that evening, they didn't use a condom.

Something unspoken passed between them the first time. As though they agreed there really was no reason to use them any longer. They were mated. It was how it should be. Should she get pregnant? Wonderful.

He entered her deeply and stayed inside, using small in and out thrusts, making her toes curl and her palms tingle. He nibbled on her neck and kissed her on the mouth, mimicking the motions of their lovemaking with his tongue. He quickened the short pulses and growled in her ear when she grabbed his ass and squeezed. With superhuman strength, he lifted her clear of the water to press against the tiled wall.

"Ah! Ah!" Every movement stole her breath. "Oh my God! Greyson!"

"Mmm. Yes, yes. Come with me, baby. Come with me!" With each *yes*, with each *come*, he plunged into her and filled her as she climaxed.

He held her there, against the wall, and ravaged her lips, her throat, her breasts. And then he sank their bodies into the hot water. Together, they sighed in ecstasy.

They laid in blissful silence, eyes closed, caressing each other. "Greyson."

"Hmm?"

"This is going to sound weird, but would you do something for me?"

"What?"

She turned in his arms so they could be face to face. "Would you look into my eyes and tell me what you see?"

He laughed.

"Don't laugh. Just do it."

"All right." He looked in her eyes. She stared, trying hard not to blink, and after a few moments, his smile melted, and his eyes welled with tears. He looked away.

"What did you see? Tell me."

"No." He sniffed and splashed his face with bathwater.

"Tell me!"

"I saw myself. My wretched self."

She nodded, knowing exactly what he meant. There was no sense in objecting and trying to change his perspective at this point when she'd felt the same way about herself. They'd need to work on their issues together, over time. "You want to know what I saw?"

"Sure."

"I saw my miserable self in your eyes, too."

"What does it mean?"

"I think our troubled souls are connected somehow. Probably by our mating. We've found them a home, but now they're seeking contentment within each other."

"You're my home, Willow."

"And you're mine, my sweet Greyson. Now to work on our contentment."

"We've got an approval to get from my Alpha and Enforcer, and I've got brothers who I now have to kill. I'm afraid contentment is a long way off."

"I'm so sorry about that horrendous find today. So very sorry. We'll get there, Greyson. And we'll get there together. I pinky swear." She held out a crooked finger. "Go on. Link yours up with mine."

"Okay." He did as she said.

"Now say pinky swear."

He chuckled. "Pinky swear."

"All right then. We're on the road to contentment, Greyson. We've sworn an oath."

"Let's dunk on it!"

"No!"

He picked her up and splashed her in the tub.

When she came up for air, she had a few choice

words for him as he ran from the bathroom. "You're dead meat! Karma's a bitch, and here she comes!"

***

"Greyson."

"Ryker." The man hadn't changed a bit from the last time they were together. Still rugged, in control, a man of succinct speech.

"Thanks for the treat you left at my door the other day."

"Thought you'd appreciate it."

"Yeah, well, Saja has a message for you." Before Greyson could ask, Ryker swatted him across the top of his head. "Don't leave dead animals on our doorstep anymore, or you're gonna be joining them."

"Damn, didn't think she'd leave the cabin before you." He rubbed his head and chuckled a bit. "Sorry it took so damn long to nab him." So far, so good. The bath he took with bleach must've worked to remove all trace of Willow's scent.

"Sometimes rogues can be difficult to track. You're a strong tracker, even though you weren't born one, and, given time, you could be one of the best."

"Thanks. That means a lot, knowing you have

that kind of faith in me."

He grunted something unintelligible as Drew walked up to where they stood by the barn door. He'd figured it would be the appropriate place to talk. "Ryker. Been a long time Grey. Too long, if you ask me, but I know you got your reasons. Good to see you."

Greyson shifted his weight from one foot to another. Only Drew could make him squirm in his shoes, but that was all right. He was his Alpha now, not a buddy, and what he had to tell him, well, it would make anyone a bit nervous. "Thanks for understanding."

"So, you called this meeting. Let's go inside and talk." The three entered the cavernous building and sat on a grouping of hay bales. "What's up?"

"I've mated." That's all he wanted to say at the moment. He'd use their reactions as a guide to see how far he could go with the details.

"I had a feeling. Can't really hide behind bleach, my friend. It's a smelly clue something's being covered up. Congratulations!" Drew clapped him on the back.

Ryker sat, stoic. Only an eyebrow raised slightly. "Really?"

Greyson smirked. "I am a hard one. I know."

"Ryker, come on, man."

"It's okay, Drew. He's only speaking the truth. Most women don't hang around very long. I've heard I'm cold and lack feelings. A couple hung around for a bit. You know, friends with benefits, but this one...she's a keeper."

"So, when do we get to meet her?"

"There's a, uh, small detail I need to share with you." He coughed and cleared his throat.

"Yes?" Ryker's unreadable expression barely shifted.

"I've mated with a human," he mumbled quickly.

"You've what?" Drew asked.

"Mated with a human," he shouted.

"Oh, for Pete's sake!" Drew pinched the bridge of his nose. "What the hell did you have to go and do that for? You see, Ryker. You set a precedent when you mated with Saja. Now you have to deal with issues like this."

"Drew, I didn't seek this out. It happened totally by accident, but I love this woman with every piece of my heart and soul. I can't live without her, and I'll protect her until my last dying breath."

"What about *her*?" Ryker challenged. Nothing in

his inflection changed, yet judgment waited in his cool eyes. "Does she have the same strong words for you? Does she know what I do to those who threaten our existence? Is she prepared to protect not only you but this pack, as well?"

"Yes, to everything."

Drew leaned forward, his expression equally intense. "What's her name? What's her profession? What are your plans? I would imagine she's living with you, wherever that is."

"Her name is Willow Bisset." He took a deep breath. Here came the dangerous part. "She used to be a fashion photographer, but her passion lies with capturing nature on film. Our plans are to travel wherever she needs to satisfy that passion."

"She's a photographer?" The air around the other man seemed to crackle.

"Patience." Drew raised his hand, yet the same question hovered around him. "She cannot photograph us, Greyson."

"I don't know much about mating, but I know I had nothing to do with my choice of mate. She has sworn an oath to me never to reveal what I am and never to take any photographs in our pack lands. That's why, for her, I'll go wherever she needs me to for her art and career."

"You swear on your life, and hers." It was the pledge all Wolves with human mates had to take. They were directly responsible for their mate's actions and their lives were forfeit if the pack could be harmed. "Are we clear?"

"Yes. Perfectly."

The Enforcer studied him, and must have found what he sought because he nodded once. "Leaving pack land could be dangerous for you." Damn, the man cared after all.

"I have to say, my first instinct is to say, no way in hell are either of you leaving." The Alpha had always cared. "But you know something, Ryker? He's different. Yes, we took him in. He's grown up as though he was a Tao, and he even works with us, but he's not Tao. I mean, he chose to live outside our boundaries as it is because he wasn't happy being under constant scrutiny. You and I both know what he had to endure while growing up. How can we blame him for wanting to get as far from here as he can? If this is his chance to be happy, I think we can make an exception for him and his mate to travel as needed for her job. Otherwise, she'd be a virtual prisoner here, not able to leave for work but not able to do her job here either. It's no way to force someone to live. I think you can appreciate the complexity here."

"As the Alpha wishes." As close to conceding a point as Ryker would likely get.

"Absolutely. Thank you both so much. I have other more disturbing news, and it's about my family."

"Your family? What the hell?"

Greyson smiled inwardly at how Drew chuffed over the mention of the woman who abandoned him.

"I was attacked a few days ago by a group of Wolves, who clearly had a bone to pick with me. It's how Willow and I came to meet. I've since found out they're my brothers. They were living with their...our mother in an abandoned shack not far from my own cabin, studying me from a distance until they were ready to attack. I'd hoped to one day meet up with her, which is why I moved to where I did, but I never imagined I'd be met with this. They tried to kill me and kidnap Willow. I killed one already. They're out for blood—mine and all who know me. I plan on going after them today and finishing them off. I want you to be on the lookout for anything suspicious. I don't know if they have others involved. I'll let you know when they are dead."

"Shit, Greyson, that's gotta fuck with your mind pretty bad. I'm sorry. You've been dealt plenty of raw deals in life so far, but this is fucked-up. It's as good as taken care of. We got this."

"Thanks, Drew, but this is a job meant for me and me alone."

"But you aren't alone. Keep that in mind. We're here not only for your protection but for the pack's as well." The Alpha reinforced the offer as he rose and offered his hand to Greyson.

Clasping it, Greyson smiled. "I know. It's time to slay my demons. Thank God I've got Willow and the pack. I'd be dead if you hadn't picked me up. I'll always be grateful, even if I do seem distant and want my privacy. Always grateful."

Ryker rose with them then clasped his hand, as well. "I'll be nearby if you need assistance." It wasn't an offer. The Enforcer had spoken, and Greyson smiled inwardly at his funny way of showing affection. "Bring the woman around some time, would ya? I think we'd all be interested in meeting her."

"Yes, I will. Once things settle down."

Not wanting to waste any time, he shifted into

his Wolf, howled his relief and joy, then ran off toward his home and mate.

***

Something felt wrong as he approached his cabin. Very wrong. His ears erect, he listened for any sounds of distress. The white fur bristled on his hackles, anticipating a sudden attack. He sniffed the air while looking around for anything amiss. The pine needles on the ground around the house weren't in the same pattern as they were when he'd left earlier, and, with no breeze, he was certain the wind had nothing to do with it. He picked up a foreign scent he sorely recognized as his brothers. He scanned the area again for any unwanted guests lurking in the background, but found none.

Had they come to scope out the place, or were they already here, inside? The probable answer made his hot blood run cold. Willow! If they so much as touched a hair on her head....

A successful rescue mission called for a cool head, so his Wolf would have to take second position for now, given the rage coursing through his veins. That kind of fury would only hinder his effectiveness, not help it. No, this operation called for the cunning of a human who knew humans. The man in him fought a hard battle for a measure of control, but he *did* win. It wasn't easy to maintain his Wolf form while thinking like a man, but he'd been practicing balancing the two within him for a little while now and he could do it successfully for about thirty minutes before one or the other took over. He'd verify his brothers were in his home and determine Willow's whereabouts and condition.

Padding over near a window, he lifted his paws to lean in and peered inside. The sons of a bitch had her. They were in Wolf form, one sitting on either side of Willow, who sat in a chair facing the front door. The third stood to the side of front door. *So, they're lying in wait for me, are they? Hoping I'll eventually come home and walk in, oblivious. Then they'll attack and kill me while my mate looks on. How predictable can they be?*

He scrutinized her position before engaging. She'd been gagged, and her hands were tied behind her chair, her feet secured to each leg. He saw no tears on her cheeks or red, watery eyes, so she hadn't been crying. *Brave girl.* Her clothes weren't askew, so they hadn't messed with her. She was simply bait and a way to make his death all the more sweet to them. They were in for a big surprise.

He scooted around to the back of the cabin and caused a bit of a ruckus with the rakes and shovels. Then he hid behind the shed as best he could, being huge. And white. As expected, a few moments later, he heard the door squeak open. One of the brothers came around...as a man. Perfect. He was playing right into his hands. The white Wolf sat patiently, waiting for the right moment. His brother bent down and reached for the handle of a shovel. That was his opening.

Greyson took a running leap and knocked Ezrah clear off his feet. While dazed and surprised, the brother left himself open to attack, giving Greyson enough time to bite and clamp down on his neck. As blood oozed out from around his teeth, gurgling sounds fueled his need for justice and retaliation. The bastard's arms and legs spasmed and flailed about. He wouldn't draw out this one's death. There wasn't time. The others inside could kill Willow at any moment. He shook his head vigorously until he heard a snap. With the neck broken, the man lay limp in the white Wolf's mouth.

"Hey, Ezrah? You all right out there? Having a

showdown with a rabbit or something? Ezrah?"

Greyson dropped the carcass to the ground and trotted behind the shed. *Come on. Come on. Be just a little too curious and stupid!*

"Ezrah?" Another brother, Kane, appeared exactly in the manner of the first. He stopped short when he noticed the body lying on the ground. He patted his waist, probably looking for a weapon, but his hands came up empty. As he started to shift, Greyson pounced, not letting the process complete itself. Not only did he bite this one, but he tore the throat clear off. He spat out the vile, coppery-tasting chunk of human flesh and knew he wouldn't get so lucky with the final slaying. He'd have to go inside to finish things.

Steeling himself, he prepared for anything to happen. He'd gotten good and bloodied by the mayhem he'd wreaked, so, first, he cleaned his muzzle in the rain barrel. Then, he shifted into his man form. He was glad Josiah was the last to die. He hoped he'd shifted out of his Wolf form. He deserved to die as a man, for the way he treated Willow. *Filthy pig scumbag!*

He stood at the base of the steps leading to the front porch and flexed his hands. When he curled them up, his fists were solid and ready to destroy. He took in a deep breath and stepped onto the first step, then the second and third. When he reached the porch, he stopped and drew in another long, steadying breath. He knew what he'd find when he opened the door. Josiah would have Willow's safety compromised. She'd either be throttled by his hands, have a knife ready to slice her throat, or she'd have a gun pointed at her head.

Best way to handle this? Just walk in. Two steps forward and he burst through the front door.

"Ah, ah, ah. Easy there, fella. I wouldn't charge one step closer if I were you. Although it doesn't really matter since you're both gonna die in a couple of minutes anyway. Come in, Greyson. Nice and easy."

He followed his orders while assessing the situation. His assumption was correct. Josiah had shifted to human form after his brothers hadn't returned. Shifting gave him more ways to inflict pain and death. He currently had his hands wrapped tightly around her throat.

"Since my brothers haven't come back, let me guess. You killed them. I don't really give a flying fuck. More for me at the dinner table. Now, you and

I, we're gonna have a little talk. And then you both are gonna die."

"I have nothing to say, except are you okay, Willow?" She blinked a couple of times, and sniffled. The tears she'd stifled to this point trickled down her cheeks in an endless stream. Seeing her so frightened and helpless to do anything shredded his heart. "So, brother, why don't you tell me what's on your mind? What's got you so sore against me you all want me dead? I mean, I didn't even know my family existed until you tried to kill me."

"You know about us being brothers? Well, that doesn't make this as much fun as me springing it on you. You, dear brother, were first of our litter to be born. Ain't it a kick in the pants? The firstborn was a runt! Mama ran you as far from our pack lands as she could and left you to die. She came back to us and everything was fine for a good long while, until we heard through channels about a white Wolf roaming the area where she dropped you. Wouldn't have mattered much except...you're Alpha. Our land technically belongs to you. It's been mine, since I came outta our mother right after you. I promised my brothers pieces of the territory if they'd help me get rid of you. Now they're gone, you're gonna be gone, and there's all that prime real estate waiting for me."

"Where is this land?"

"Washington, far southeast corner. So far, we've gone undetected, unlike the regular Wolf packs all over the state. I basically have hundreds of miles with not even another Wolf pack to bother us."

"How big is the pack?"

"We're small. About a hundred of us. Now, ninety-seven, thanks to you."

His mind was officially blown. He was born an Alpha? He had a pack? And land? And this asshole wanted to keep it all to himself. He found he stood a bit taller, like a switch in his brain turned on and Alpha tendencies and instinct kicked in. "Where's our mother now? Does she know I'm alive, or did you keep it a secret from her?"

"Oh, she knows. But I'm her pride and joy. You're the runt she wished never was born and hoped would die."

Ouch. Just a little. But it was nothing new. The pain from that kind of rejection never went away. "Well, I can't let you get away with this, you know. And, you've got my mate in a precarious position, which I can't allow either. So, stop hiding behind a woman and come outside where you can challenge my position properly." He knew the "woman" comment would stir him up, and hoped he'd take him on.

"All right, Mr. I'm All That. I'll show you who's the real Alpha here." Willow's eyes widened and her face reddened. She shook in her chair like a moth caught in a spider's web. The bastard was choking her! And Greyson couldn't do a damn thing, yet, or risk causing her death. "Relax, pretty lady. Just putting you to sleep. Sleep." He released her throat, but his handprints remained and her head slumped to her chest. A satisfied grin swallowed up his face. "You see? Who's the Alpha here? Me!"

He stepped aside and shifted into his Wolf.

"You'll pay." Greyson shifted, as well, and they grappled with each other until they tumbled out the front door onto the porch and down the steps.

Josiah was built slightly bigger than the other three, so presented Greyson his only true challenge of the day. He raised up on his hind legs and attacked, but only managed to nip Greyson's muzzle. Standing up on his own hind legs, he was a good head and shoulders taller than his traitorous brother. He bared his teeth, dripping with intent to do serious bodily damage, and then he sank them into the other Wolf's shoulder.

Back and forth they went, trading bites and gouges with their claws until Greyson found an opening and went straight for the kill. He held onto his brother's neck, shaking it every couple of seconds, heedless of the yowling and slow trickle of blood seeping out of the puncture wounds. This victory tasted the sweetest. He tightened his jaw, crunching into fat, muscle, and, at last, bone.

Dead. His brothers were all dead. Thanks to their greed and their mother's rejection of him.

He let go of Josiah. Dropped him right at his own feet. A gift to himself, the new Alpha. He howled and bayed a few times, stuck his snout into the rain barrel to clean up and remove the foul taste of the bastard, then rushed inside to see to Willow. He barked and trotted circles around her. Her head still rested on her chest. He nudged her chin with his muzzle and chuffed. Still, he got no response. So he shifted into his human form.

"Willow, wake up, please." He removed the gag from her mouth then checked for a pulse to see if she still breathed. She was alive. Josiah had probably put a blood choke on her, causing her to pass out. He held her face in his trembling hands and kissed her lips, forcing every positive thought he had into her. Untying her, he lifted her from the chair and sat on the couch with her resting in his arms. The thought of having to live the rest of his life without her was unacceptable. If she didn't revive, he'd go find her in the next life.

A moan. He thought he heard a moan! "Willow! Wake up! Come back to me!"

Her eyes fluttered open, and she took in a deep breath. "Greyson?" she croaked. "Is it over? Are we safe?"

"Yes, it's over."

"Oh, thank God." More alert, she slid her arms around his thick waist and nestled in. He wrapped his own around her and pulled her closer still. No prompting necessary.

"You were so brave. I'm so sorry my family's done this to you."

She peered up at him and caressed his cheek. "Don't apologize for them. They weren't your family. They just shared your DNA. Family is your pack. Me."

He leaned down and laid his lips softly against hers, hoping doing so conveyed how very right he thought she was. Her hand slid behind his neck and pulled him closer as she deepened his kiss. That one led to more, and the situation heated up quickly. Willow rearranged herself to straddle him and pulled his shirt off. Amidst a flurry of frenetic kisses, she squirmed against him, causing his pants to feel quite constricted.

"Greyson, I need you, baby. Right now." She reached down and unzipped his jeans, and, of course, he'd gone commando again, so his hardened shaft was ready and waiting. He pulled his pants down a bit more to free himself, and she wasted no time in pleasuring him with her warm, silky mouth and wicked tongue.

As she licked him from base to tip, he shivered and groaned and grabbed fistfuls of her long, flowing hair. He didn't have to guide her. She knew exactly what to do. He needed to touch her, any part of her. She focused on the tip and sucked on him while pumping the rest of the shaft with her hand. He growled low and knew he wasn't far from climaxing. He released her hair and leaned forward to grab her onto his lap. He didn't know when she'd done it, but she was bare-assed when he raised her up.

He slid his hands under and felt her heat. He stroked her a few times and thrust a finger inside her. When he pulled it out, he brought it to his nose and mouth and sucked on it. He loved the smell and taste of his mate. Like the sweetest candy. Breathing heavily, he lifted her up and slid her down on him once, twice, and kept her there. She rocked on him as he removed her shirt and bra and made love to her breasts.

"You're so perfect. So beautiful. So...everything to me, Willow baby."

Her moans and cries filled the space around them as she grabbed onto the edge of the couch and started pumping up and down on him, faster and faster. Forehead to forehead, breaths colliding, they came together and she collapsed against his chest.

"Stay inside me as long as you can. You feel too good."

"I'm not moving." He caressed her back, making little circles from her shoulders to the base of her spine, and then held her in quiet reverence.

Chapter Seven

"No! My boys! My boys!" A wail, like a banshee came from outside, startling Greyson awake. He hadn't realized he'd fallen asleep. "No!"

"Shit," Greyson muttered, scrubbing his face. He maneuvered Willow, who'd dozed off, as well, onto the couch. He lowered his voice to a whisper. "Get dressed. Stay here. Don't make a sound or come outside." She nodded and pulled on her clothes as he did the same.

"Why? Why?" His mother's pain-filled sobbing continued as he stepped onto the porch. She was kneeling over Josiah's body, her back facing him. "My dear boys!"

"You still have one left, Mother." He walked down the stairs with all the swagger of a man wronged.

She whipped around, revealing a horrified expression and crazed eyes. She stood and pointed a shaky finger at him. "You! You! I should have killed you myself and not left it up to nature! Look what you've done! You've killed my family!"

"Great to see you, too. Never mind the fact they came here to kill me first."

"You were already dead. So what? Now, now I go home with no family, no Alpha. But at least I'll go with the knowledge that I killed the slayer of our leader!"

With her proclamation, she pulled a gun on him from under her shirt. She fired immediately, but the bullet whizzed by without doing any damage. She fired again, but she lacked aim due to her crazed, maniacal behavior. She'd be out of bullets before she could get one close to grazing him.

He moved in on her, preparing to wrestle the gun away. She fired another shot. Three more to go. Still no closer to hitting him than before. Still he approached, until he was close enough grab the gun.

"No! Let go! You can't be our Alpha. You're a runt, a freak of nature. That's all you are! Ah!"

She had horrible aim, but was stronger than she looked, hanging on to the gun as though it were glued to her hands. She tried to maneuver the muzzle so it dug into his body, but, as in arm wrestling, he was able to push it aside and down.

"You must die!" She gave it all she had, and the gun went off.

He froze, waiting to feel telltale pain come from *some*where. But it didn't. He looked down at his mother and found a seething anger directed toward him. It shot through his soul worse than any bullet could. Her hand released the gun, and she crumbled to the ground, blood spurting from her leg.

She gazed up at him, disgust and disdain in her pale-amber eyes, and spoke in a cold, clear voice. "From the minute you were born I never wanted you. I never loved you. You weren't supposed to live. And now, you'll have everything that belonged to me and my family. That's the thanks I get for weeding out the weak and keeping the pack strong. Such cruel irony. I hate you. I don't even know your name, and I hate you."

Blood continued to gush and pool around her thigh, and she toppled over unconscious. Those were the last words she spoke to her firstborn son.

He stood above her, stoic at first, as he watched the woman's life drain from her body. He had no frame of reference to think about what kind of mother she could have been or what kind of life he could have had, had he been normal. His life was what it was, and he was okay with it. Even better, now that Willow was in it.

His family had come, invaded his territory, sullied his home, and wanted him dead. He'd fought and won. But at what cost? He'd only ever killed Wolves as a Wolf. He'd never killed anyone, animal or human, as a human. It felt like murder. It *was* murder. He'd murdered his mother. Yes, she was a stranger, and a hateful one to boot, but she was still his mother. He turned his palms up and looked at them. Could there have been any other outcome? Probably not. It didn't make it hurt any less. For the first time, he saw himself as a monster. How apropos he should feel like that while being human.

He released a howl so long and mournful to his own ears, he covered them.

He turned away from his mother to glance at his future back in the cabin and saw Willow standing in the doorway. Her eyes sought to understand what she could do to help, but he had no answer for her. She opened her arms to him, and a short, high-pitched whine escaped his lips as he realized what he desperately needed. Simply her. Each step he took felt like a step toward redemption and acceptance.

She met him halfway, and he dropped to his knees before her. His arms snaked around her body to hold her close. He kissed her belly and closed his eyes as she stroked his hair. Cared for, cherished, for the first time in his life.

"Willow...."

"My baby. My sweet baby. I'm here. I love you. I'm here, and I'm not going anywhere."

"What I've done—"

"What you've done, you had to do. You saved me. You saved yourself. You saved your pack. Be proud. Don't let the ugliness of your birth family mar the richness of the life you've had and *can* have with me."

She knelt with him and held his face in her hands. "Look into my eyes, Greyson, and tell me what you see. Look!"

He obeyed, and was shocked. "I...I see my soul joined with yours."

"I do, too. What does that tell you?"

"This is right. We're meant to complete each other."

"And we can handle anything, together. No more hiding under hoods, behind sunglasses, or in self-imposed exile. No more settling for less than what we want out of life. Together, we are a force to be reckoned with."

"Yes. Yes, we are." With everything that had happened, he hadn't had the chance to tell her the news. "And we have Drew and Ryker's approval."

"Really? We're okay? We have their blessings?"

"Yes. We have to swear an oath of secrecy. We can stay here. We can go whenever and wherever we want."

"That's wonderful!"

"There's something else. Something rather...life-altering."

"Even more so than this?" She scoffed.

"Let's go inside, and I'll tell you all about it."

***

"Everything packed up, locked up, and ready to go?"

"Ready, Captain!" Willow shouted from the passenger seat of her truck. She had her hair pulled up in a high ponytail, exposing what Greyson considered the juiciest part of her throat.

He hopped in the driver's side and started the

engine. Then he nibbled on the fleshy part of her neck and moved on to kiss her full on the mouth. There was no sating his desire for her now that they'd mated, and he loved it. "Then let's move on out!"

Greyson took a last glance at his cabin, now all boarded up like a vacation home. They wouldn't be back for a while. They'd said their good-byes to everyone last night at a huge feast in town. Betty had cried and hugged him over and over again. Drew had sat him down earlier in the day and imparted many words of wisdom that would help him tremendously on his journey. In return, Greyson, swore an additional oath to Drew that, if and when he returned to Los Lobos, he would never try to usurp Drew's position. He would relinquish his own Alpha status in deference to Drew. When the evening was over, Willow and he thanked everyone for their kindness and promised they'd come back to visit before anyone missed them.

He grabbed Willow's hand and kissed her palm, then held it in his lap as he pulled out onto the dirt road. "Have I told you lately how much I love you?"

"Not since five minutes ago." Her eyes sparkled. He loved how they did that whenever he told her he loved her, which he'd taken to doing a lot.

"Then I'm overdue. My apologies. I love you, sweet Willow, with every breath and snarl I have in this imperfect body."

"And I love you, my sweet Greyson, with every white and red blood cell in my body."

He chuckled and leaned over to kiss her. He put the truck into gear and put his foot on the gas pedal. "Look out, Washington! There's a new Alpha comin' to town."

About the Author

My name is Deena Remiel, and I am an author of paranormal romance, urban and dark fantasy, and romantic suspense. I also teach language arts to middle schoolers. I belong to RWA national and the Desert Rose Chapter of RWA, where there are outstanding people writing fabulous stories.

I grew up in Philadelphia, home of the most amazing cheese steaks, soft pretzels, oh and the Liberty Bell. My husband and I began our own family in New Jersey, and just a few years ago, Arizona called to my spirit and tempted my husband with much better weather! We moved our family, and the rest is history, or the present, as the case may be!

These are a few of my favorite things: writing and reading of course, chocolate, music with lyrics or melodies that speak to me, soaking baths, singing in the shower, dancing with my buds, romantic dancing with my hubbie, scrapbooking, watching my girls enjoy what they love to do, and laughing at jokes. Visit my website for the latest news and available books: www.deenaremiel.com.

Feel free to contact me: deenaremiel@yahoo.com